Indelibly Inked

Jamie DeBree

Indelibly Inked
ISBN 9781937477684
Indelibly Inked Copyright © 2012 Jamie M DeBree
Published by Brazen Snake Books

Edited by Carol R. Ward

Also by the Author

Tempest

Desert Heat

The Biker's Wench

The Minister's Maid

Heart Knocks

Chapter One

Claire parked her car at the curb and stared at the blue neon letters that spelled out "Indelible Ink" across a dark window. She got out, her stomach fluttering at the thought of what she was about to do. Stacy had insisted it was necessary. She'd even made an after-hours appointment with the owner to avoid any bad publicity before the press conference. Claire still wasn't convinced. It was such a small thing. Who would even notice?

She rapped twice on the door, surprised when it swung open right away. There were no lights on in the shop and she hadn't noticed anyone on the other side of the glass. She stepped inside, unable to see anything but the profile of a tall, apparently well-built man in the dim storefront. A sliver of light drew her gaze down a long hall, and she assumed that was where they'd be working. Heat flooded through her as the man's warm, spicy scent enveloped her senses. Suddenly she was grateful for the darkness, embarrassed at her reaction. Obviously it had been too long since she'd been this close to a man.

A real one, anyway.

"Thank you for meeting me after hours," she said, anxious to break the silence.

He closed the door and secured the deadbolt with a loud click. "It's okay," he said. His voice was low and rough, sending another prickle of awareness over her senses. "I've got a room set up back here, if you want to come with me."

Boy do I.

She followed him down the hall, focusing on his back as it came into focus closer to the light. Well-defined muscles stretched his black t-shirt tight and she fought the urge to run her fingers over the lines. It had definitely been too long.

An exam table complete with a paper cover sat under a bright spotlight in the back room. He stepped over to a counter on the far wall and washed his hands while she hung her coat and purse on a hook beside the door. "Go ahead and hop up there," he said, opening a drawer. She gave an awkward little jump to hoist herself onto the table as he snapped on a pair of white latex gloves.

"I really don't think it was necessary to sneak around, but my publicist thought…"

She lost her train of thought the second his eyes

met hers. Steel gray and cool, there was something so familiar about them that she couldn't look away. She struggled to remember what she'd been saying, heat flooding her face as he stepped closer to the table.

"You'll need to slide up more - it's on your ankle, right?"

The question startled her. "Um, yes. Sorry." She moved farther up, until just her feet were hanging over the edge. He slid her high heel off and she froze as he reached out to gently grasp her right foot. She turned it out to reveal a small image on the inside of her ankle.

"Let's see what you've got." His touch was gentle as he ran a finger over the tattoo she'd gotten so long ago. She couldn't see it clearly from her position, but in her mind she saw the small stylized tree inked into her skin, a heart in the center bearing two sets of initials. A talisman from another time.

His hands were warm as he gently rotated her leg, his brows drawn together as he examined the image. "Nice tat. Who did the original work?" He glanced up, and she smiled.

"Bailey's on Fourth Street," she said. "Nathan Bailey did it for me. My best friend had a crush on him back then. She, uh…dared me to get the tattoo."

He nodded, and ran a finger over her skin once more. She fought a shiver from his touch. "It's nice work. Who's the lucky guy? Or unlucky, I guess, considering why we're here."

She laughed, feeling the blush was creep higher on her cheeks. "It was a guy I had a huge crush on in high school. It sounds silly now, but he sort of inspired me to do more - to want more out of life."

"So what went wrong?"

She shrugged, giving him a sheepish grin. "He...ah...he barely knew I was alive, to be honest. We weren't exactly in the same social set." Or on the same planet, for that matter, she mused silently. He'd been rich, the son of a senator. There was no doubt in her mind that his parents wouldn't have approved of him dating the daughter of a strung-out stripper.

"But you inked his initials on your ankle." It wasn't a question, and Claire just nodded, avoiding eye contact. She'd never told anyone the story before, and after tonight it wouldn't matter anyways. Still, she blinked back sudden tears that threatened to spill over. He laid his hand casually over her calf and she could feel him watching her. That feeling that she'd met him before tugged at the edges of her memory.

She looked at him again, focusing on the lines of his face. They'd definitely met before, and she frowned. He must not recognize her. "Have we-"

"So you want me to cover this up?" He spoke quickly, and she wondered if it was just bad timing, or something else.

She nodded again. "I'm announcing my candidacy for Mayor tomorrow. Stacy - my publicist - thinks that some curious person will notice the initials and start digging into my background. She's afraid of the impact it might have on my campaign if people start wondering who the mystery guy is."

"I see." He turned back to the counter, a chill moving over her skin when his hand left her ankle. "And you're willing to give this up for politics? Seems like you have a lot of history with this guy, whether he knows it or not."

She shrugged. "I don't really see the problem, personally. I'm the only one who knows who he is for sure, and I'm not talking. I have far bigger skeletons in my closet to worry about." She blinked back the sudden moisture building in her eyes. "But Stacy says that's the point - get rid of the small problems so we can focus on the bigger ones."

"Seems kind of backwards to me," he said, handing her a plastic sleeve holding a sheet of design sketches. "You have a couple of choices here," he said, his matter-of-fact tone helping her regain control. "I can work the lettering into a vine or some flowers - you can pick something from this sheet." She glanced at it. The images were well drawn, but generic. Somehow it didn't seem right to cover up something so symbolic with leaves or flowers.

He tapped her tattoo firmly with his index finger, bringing her attention back to him. He looked straight into her eyes, a challenge reflected in his stare. "Or I can touch this up for you, make the lines crisp, add a little color, and you can keep your inspiration intact.

Might not be such a good idea to mess with something like this." He raised his eyebrows, pinning her with his gaze. It was like he could see into her mind, knew all the questions and desires swirling like fireflies in her brain.

She broke eye contact, looking down at her ankle. When she'd taken Jenny's dare, she never imagined what an impact that afternoon would have on her life. Now it had brought her back to the starting point, to the same decision with far bigger things at stake. Did she dare hold on to the past, or was it time to let go of her girlish dreams?

* * *

Adam struggled to keep his hands off Claire Taylor's skin as she considered his offer. It was obvious that she wanted to keep the tattoo, and he wondered how it would affect her decision if he'd introduced himself. It had been a long time. He'd been surprised to see the hint of remembrance in her eyes. Everyone he grew up with always marveled at how much he'd changed from the skinny, geeky looking kid he had been in high school. No one recognized him right away and that was fine with him. He wanted nothing to do with his old life, filled with his father's political campaigns and keeping up appearances.

"I'll keep it." Her voice trembled slightly, and she shifted on the table, the paper cover crackling loudly.

He held back a grin and gave a curt nod, allowing his fingers to brush her ankle once more.

"Let me just do a quick touch-up," he said, peering down at the image again. The lines were a little blurred, and the colors faded from years of wear. He turned to the counter and started prepping his tools. "On the house." Paper rustling behind him made him turn to see her scooting off the edge of the table. She didn't look at him as she poked her foot back into its demure navy shoe.

"I appreciate the offer, but I really shouldn't take any more of your time." She went to the door and reached for her coat, tossing it over her arm before looking back, a shy smile on her lips. "I really should get home and run through my speech again before bed."

She slung her purse over her shoulder too hard, almost dropping her coat. He leaned a hip against the counter, watching her nervous movements and the telltale blush rising up in her cheeks again. This was the girl from high school, unpolished and adorably clumsy. He'd always watched out for her back then, even though he was too afraid of his father to make a move. He wished he'd done things differently back then.

She turned to go and her heel caught on the threshold, sending her sprawling into the hall with a yelp.

Adam ran to her side, kneeling down as she started to push herself up. "Are you okay?" She sat up and he reached for her hand to help her stand.

"Ow." She cringed as she got to her feet, holding her right foot slightly off the ground. "These stupid shoes," she said, wiggling her foot out of the offending article. "Stacy says I have to wear heels if I want to look professional. I honestly don't know how women walk in them every day without breaking their necks." She put her foot down again, wincing when she put her weight on it. "My toe is sprained, I think. Damn."

"Hold on." Adam bent and curled an arm under her knees, sweeping her off her feet. She gasped, her arms automatically circling his neck as he carried her back to the table. He liked the feel of her in his embrace - too much. He set her down gently, heat tracks scoring his skin through his shirt as her hands slid slowly off his shoulders. Her wide eyes mirrored the same confusion and longing that he felt, but he stepped back, resisting the urge to claim her lips as he should have done years ago.

"I have some ice in the back." He walked away, wondering who needed it more as hot awareness pulsed through his body.

* * *

Claire shivered as Adam put a bag of ice on her ankle a few minutes later. She bit her bottom lip, wondering how she could have missed it before. When he'd held her in his arms, pressed against his body, she'd finally recognized him. It felt the same as it had on prom night, when he'd saved her from Blake Halverson under the bleachers. He'd knocked Blake out, then carried her back to his car and drove her home. It was one of the only times she'd felt safe with a boy, and she'd wanted to cling to him, promise him anything to stay with her, just like her mom always did with men. But she'd kept quiet, not wanting to be one of *those* women, and after that night he'd kept his distance. She'd watched him though, and vowed to rise to his level someday.

"Too cold?"

She jumped at the sound of his voice. "I...uh...it's fine." She studied his profile as he prodded her foot with a finger. It was strangely disappointing to think that he hadn't even recognized her name, she thought. Apparently the connection she'd felt back then really had been one-sided, though she wasn't sure she could say the same about this particular meeting. Did he feel it too? She looked up to find him watching her carefully, an odd look on his face.

"Claire..."

Her heart sped up as she waited for him to continue. Did he know who she was? She held her breath. He was going to ask about the initials. Her mind frantically searched for an alternate name to give him, some explanation other than a silly high school crush.

"...I don't want to alarm you, but I think you might have broken a couple of toes."

She frowned, trying to switch gears as she peered down at her foot. He moved the bag of ice enough so that she could see the last two toes, bright red and swelling up like mini sausages. She realized they were numb, and tried to move them. A cry escaped her lips as white-hot pain shot through her foot and up her sore ankle as her whole body tensed in agony.

"Dang, that hurts," she said, gulping deep breaths of air as the pain slowly subsided. She felt the ice being moved closer to her toes, and blinked up at the ceiling several times to control the tears trying to escape. She looked back at Adam, who appeared to be trying not to laugh.

She frowned again. "What? You think me breaking two toes is funny? Wait until you hear from my lawyers, buddy. You won't be laughing then."

He held his hands up in surrender. "I'm just surprised at your word choice, is all. I'd have been cussing up a storm." He opened a drawer behind him, and took out medical tape and scissors. "I assume you'd rather not go to the hospital for this?"

She looked at the items, then back at her toes, still covered by the bag of melting ice. "Won't they need to do x-rays to make sure they're broken? Put a cast on my foot?" He pulled the bag away, revealing her toes again. She cringed. That wasn't the color toes were supposed to be, and was the little one supposed to be angled like that?

"I think it's pretty obvious they're broken, don't you? We'll have to straighten that little one out..." He handed her a glass of water and some pills. "It's ibuprofen - trust me, you'll need it." She swallowed them and he took the glass out of her hand, setting it on the counter. "You might want to grab the edges of the table there..."

Claire panicked as he took her foot in one hand and moved to grasp her little toe in his fingers. "Wait! What are you doing? Shouldn't we call...aaiiieeee!" Searing pain shot through her body and Claire felt faint as the world started to spin. Bright light flashed white before her eyes, and then everything faded to black.

* * *

Adam pulled Claire's mangled digit straight, a twinge of guilt striking him as he saw the fear in her eyes. Relieved that she'd fainted, he quickly wrapped the toe with gauze and medical tape to keep it straight. He anchored the other toe to the healthy one next to it and put a fresh bag of ice on it to help with the swelling. Claire was starting to come around, and he went around the table to her side. "Hey there," he said, touching her shoulder lightly. She blinked, her green eyes glistening up at him. The confusion cleared away and she struggled to sit up.

"Ow...what the heck did you do? God that hurts!" She sucked in one breath, then another as she glared at him. "Why didn't you just let me call Stacy? She could have taken me to the hospital, where they have painkillers and everything." She slid to the edge of the table, her arms poised to take her weight as she started sliding to her feet.

Adam reached her in two strides, his thick chest even with her head. "Not so fast there - you need to stay off of those toes for a few days. And your ankle needs to rest too." She tilted her head back to look up at him, and he couldn't help staring at her full, moist lips for a few seconds. He wondered how she would taste if he ran his tongue over them. He leaned in, watching her face flush with desire as she waited.

He closed his eyes, felt her breath on his skin, the warmth of her body as he pulled her closer.

"Ow...ow ow. Damn." She pushed hard against his chest and he stepped back, hands in the air. Her face was lined with pain and she took a deep breath in, her eyes scrunched tightly closed.

He looked down at her foot and he realized he must have bumped it with his leg. "Damn - I'm sorry. I shouldn't have..." He ran a hand through his hair, thinking. Ever since high school he'd wanted to kiss her, and she hadn't objected until he hit her foot. But the timing was all wrong again. A fling with him could ruin her campaign, and he still didn't want anything to do with politics.

"I...um...should probably go home." He looked up at her quiet words. Her face was still deathly pale, but she appeared to have the pain under control for the moment. "If you hand me my phone, I'll call Stacy to come and get me. I don't think I can work the gas pedal like this." One side of her mouth turned up in a wry smirk and his jeans got a little tighter at the view. He needed to get away from her, but it didn't look like that was going to happen anytime soon, unfortunately.

He got her purse off the counter and handed it to her. He knew all too well that she was probably in for a lecture from her publicist on the way home. He put his hand over her phone just before she could dial. "I'll take you home," he said, knowing it was a bad idea the moment the words came out. "Then you won't have to deal with the fallout until tomorrow."

"I don't think that's such a good idea," she said, her finger moving over the buttons. "I really should let her know what's going on, and see how this is going to affect my campaign." Her hand was shaking as she held the device to her ear, and she turned her head, refusing to make eye contact.

Adam stepped back, propped his hip against the counter and folded his arms across his chest. She was right. This one setback could require big changes in everything from her announcement tomorrow to her clothing choices. Her publicist was going to earn every cent Claire was paying her.

A soft beep drew his gaze back to her. She put the phone back in her purse and shrugged. "Stacy isn't answering," she said. A worried look crossed her face. "She always answers her phone - even in the middle of the night. She said she was going over to the hotel to check the meeting room again and then straight home from there." She frowned, and Adam longed to smooth the wrinkle from between her brows.

He settled for swinging her up off the table and into his arms. She gasped and locked her hands around his neck, her purse somehow still cradled in her lap. "What are you doing?"

"Taking you home." He carried her into the hall and out the back door, lowering her to stand on her good foot beside his black Nova. He wondered if she would remember the last time he'd driven her home, in this same car. She was quiet as he opened the passenger door and helped her slide across the front bench seat. When he finally dared a glance at her she was running one hand over the seat, a thoughtful, almost sad look on her face. Was she remembering?

"If you put your foot up on the seat, it shouldn't throb quite so much." She obediently swung her leg up towards the door, sliding closer to him. Awareness slid over his body as she brushed his shoulder, quickly drawing back. He started the engine, and hoped that her place was close. He needed to get some distance. The sooner the better.

"Where do you--"

"Can we stop at--"

She started to speak at the same time he did, and he gestured for her to go on as he backed the car out of the parking lot.

"I was just wondering if we could stop by the hotel and see if Stacy's still there. It's not like her to ignore my call. I'm worried - what if something happened?"

"Sure," Adam said, turning toward The Beaumont, the largest hotel in town. Political candidates always booked press conferences there. It was the only venue large enough for the purpose.

"I'm sure she's fine. Maybe she had a date or something." He was starting to guess that maybe this Stacy was the same one his brother had dated his senior year of high school. He hadn't recognized her voice on the phone, but he hadn't spent much time with her. If it was Stacy Newell, she hadn't been picky about men. At least not enough to keep her from sleeping with several members of the football team when David had been helping out with their father's campaigns.

Claire shook her head as he pulled into the parking lot. "She doesn't date." He found a spot and put the car in park, leaving the engine on.

"Ever? Did--is she married?" He almost bit his tongue on the wrong word, forgetting for a minute that he wasn't supposed to recognize Claire.

"No." Claire peered through the windshield at the tall, dim windows. "I think our room is that one," she said, pointing to the center door. "If you'll just help me out..."

Adam shook his head. "I'll go. You stay and keep your foot up." Not wanting to hear any protests, he got out and shut the door, quickly striding to the nearest entrance. He let himself into the dark conference room and saw a small beam of light coming from a door near the front. He started to call out, but something made him hesitate. He skirted the edge of the room until he was just outside, low voices just barely audible behind the heavy divider curtain. He leaned in to listen.

"I can't do that to her. I won't," a woman hissed.

"You don't have a choice. Either follow the plan, or your little secret is out."

It was another woman who spoke, someone who sounded very much like his mother. What would she want with Stacy, and what kind of secret could they possibly share? From what he remembered, David had never even introduced the two. High heels clicked across the floor on the other side of the wall, and he assumed one of the women was leaving. But which one?

He took a few steps back from the door, then called out. "Stacy? Are you in here?"

Shadows moved into the light as someone poked her head out the door, squinting into the darkness.

Yep. Definitely Stacy Newell. He felt like he was being dragged back in time.

"Who's out there?"

Adam moved forward, into the beam so she could see him. "Adam - from Indelibly Inked. You hired me to do some work for Claire Taylor. I was driving her home, and she wanted to check on you. Is everything okay?"

"Of course it is." Her voice was tight but professional. "Why wouldn't it be?" She looked over his shoulder, leaning out to survey the space behind him. "Where is Claire? And why are you taking her home?"

She fidgeted nervously, taking a step away from him. This was not the Stacy he remembered. She still looked the same, but there was a haunted, wary look in her eyes. Had his mother put it there?

He backed off a step, hoping to put her at ease.

"She can't drive at the moment. She fell on those high-heeled shoes and broke two toes. When she couldn't reach you, I told her I'd take her home."

"Oh god - I must have left my phone in the car." She checked her watch. "It's so late too. I need to get home."

Adam waited, knowing it was going to hit her any second.

Her eyes widened suddenly, and she reached out to steady herself on the back of a chair. "Did you say she broke two toes?"

"'Fraid so."

Stacy shook her head. "This night can't possibly get any worse. Did she recognize you?" He shook his head, wondering why she'd made the appointment with him if she'd known who he was all along. Something definitely wasn't right in all this.

"Stacy? Are you okay?"

They both turned to see Claire hobbling slowly up the center aisle of chairs, her face pale in the darkness.

Chapter Two

Claire let out a long breath as she finally reached the front of the room where Stacy and Adam were waiting. She slid onto the nearest chair, willing the pain in her foot away. She'd underestimated the logistics of walking barefoot, with two freshly-broken toes, over the pavement and now the nerves in both feet were firing off with wild abandon.

Stacy rushed to her side, kneeling down to examine Claire's bandaged foot. "I'm fine - but what happened to you?"

"I fell off those stupid heels," she said, noting the frown Stacy shot at Adam. "It's not his fault. I was in a hurry and didn't watch where I was going. He...um...set my toes."

Stacy looked up, her eyes wide. "He what?" She turned to Adam, her brows drawn. "Why didn't you take her to the hospital?"

"Didn't think you'd want the publicity, what with the big campaign and all."

Stacy shook her head. "Just because that's what your dad would have done..." She glanced down at Claire and pressed her lips together.

"Don't bother." Claire looked up at Adam. She saw it in his eyes - recognition mixed with a hint of guilt. Just how long had he known? She turned back to Stacy. "Apparently we all know who's who. No more games. What's going on here?"

Stacy tucked a stray hair behind her ear then checked her watch. She turned to Adam. "I don't have much time, but I was hoping maybe you could help us out. Claire may be in danger."

"What kind of danger?" Claire asked, wincing as she stood. She quickly shifted her weight to her left foot as Adam took a step toward her. "Why didn't you tell me before?"

"I didn't think it was serious until yesterday." Stacy shrugged. "Political candidates get threats all the time. But I think there might be something to this."

Adam reached up and rubbed his neck with one hand. "Why me?"

"Yeah, why him?" Claire glared at her in the darkened room. "You made the appointment - you insisted that I had to go to his shop. Why?"

Stacy reached down for the portfolio on the table at her side. "I knew he'd take care of you - or I hoped he would. You two seemed to have a...connection in high school. Claire trusts you, or she did once." She looked pointedly at Adam then started walking toward the door.

"Hey wait - what's he supposed to protect me from? And what are we going to do about tomorrow?" Claire curled her fingers around the back of a chair, wanting to run after her campaign manager but knowing she couldn't. She didn't dare look at the would-be protector standing silently beside her.

Stacy glanced over her shoulder. "I'll call you first thing tomorrow morning. Don't stay alone tonight, okay?" She turned and walked out, leaving Claire to wonder if she really would call.

Suddenly the room felt very small as Adam stepped closer. She forced herself to look at him, her heart beating fast. He knew who she was - and that meant he must know that those were his initials on her ankle. There was no more pretending, her infatuation was finally out in the open after all these years.

She met his eyes, expecting to find anger or betrayal. There was no judgment though, only a calmness that confused her after the heat that had been reflected there earlier. Embarrassed, she dropped her gaze to the floor, thankful for the darkness that hid the color rising over her cheeks.

"I'm really sorry about all this," she said, her voice low. "If you wouldn't mind driving me home, I can deal with all of this tomorrow." She started limping toward the door, not really wanting a reply of any sort. It was unbelievable that Stacy had tried to manipulate him - both of them - like this. She fought back tears as she pushed open the door to the hall, careful not to hit her toes on the way out. She'd have to withdraw from the race. She couldn't go forward with a publicist she couldn't trust, and the threat of personal danger looming over her head.

She stopped at the door to the parking lot, staring at the hard pavement. Maybe she should just get a room here tonight. She turned back, only to find herself staring at Adam's strong, broad chest.

"Oh," she gasped, a nervous giggle escaping her lips. "I didn't know you were so close behind me. Maybe I should just get a room here tonight. Then you wouldn't have to go out of your way and I'll be here early tomorrow." She tried to step back, but the door was right behind her. His expression was almost amused as he took a single step forward.

"Your publicist seems to think you shouldn't be alone," he said, bracing a hand on the door above her head. "And I think maybe we have some things to discuss."

Claire silently reminded herself to breathe, drawing in the warm, earthy fragrance of the man towering over her. She averted her eyes and looked for something - anything else to focus on rather than his piercing gaze.

"I'd rather just go to bed. I'm really tired." She opened her mouth to fake a yawn that turned out to be the real thing. Tilting her head to the side, she peeked up at him with what she hoped was a coy little smile. Sometimes her mother's moves came in handy, though Claire was convinced that her IQ dropped every time she used one. "Would you mind if we talked tomorrow? It's been a long day, and my foot really hurts--"

"I don't think so, Princess." Adam leaned in close and bent down, his lips grazing hers ever so lightly. She closed her eyes as he grasped her wrists and guided her hands to his neck. His silk-soft hair tickled her fingers. She pulled him closer, opening her mouth to allow him better access. A low moan sent tremors through her skin and a delicious heat buzzing through her core.

He nuzzled in, pressing kisses down the length of her neck. She whimpered as his mouth left her skin and opened her eyes as he lifted her in his arms for the third time that night. She'd have to remember to thank her mother, she thought. After they checked in.

A satisfied smirk played at his lips. He shouldered the door open again, and carried her back to his car. She frowned up at him, confused. "Where are we going? I thought...I mean..." She searched for the right words as he set her on her feet and opened the door. "Are you taking me home?" She got in and pulled her feet up, still hazy from his kiss. He closed her door and walked around to slid behind the wheel.

"We'll go to my place," he said, pulling out of the

hotel parking lot. "It's close. You'll be safe there."

She studied his profile in the darkness. His face was all hard angles, the high cheekbones and sharp nose reminiscent of an ancient gladiator. His eyes were deep-set, his mouth full and wide. His hair was cut in a straight shag that just touched the base of his neck and hung down over his left eye, somehow managing to look neat and rebellious at the same time.

She licked her lips, wondering how she hadn't recognized him right away. Even with the obvious hours he'd spent in the weight room and the bad-boy hair style, his face was the same, just more mature. So were the shadows she saw behind his eyes whenever he looked at her.

He turned into the driveway of a smallish brick house and shut off the engine.

"Stay there for a minute." The stern command was softened by a slight break in his voice. Claire watched him open the door and disappear inside. A soft light came on in the front window. What was he doing? She grinned at the thought of him hastily picking up his bachelor pad. A couple of minutes later, he jogged back to the car and opened her door.

"These will be a little big, but they'll protect your feet." He held out a pair of fleece-lined leather slippers.

"Um...thanks." Claire slipped them on, wincing a little as her toes slid down into the cozy lining. She reached up to take his offered hand, careful not to put much weight on her injured foot.

"Much better." She smiled, but he appeared to be looking at something on the other side of the car. She glanced at the bushes lining his driveway. The night suddenly seemed very still - almost eerie. She shivered.

"Good." Adam shut the door behind her then gestured toward the house. "Can you walk on your own? I need to get something out of the garage, but the front door is open."

He wasn't going to carry her again? Claire nodded, annoyed at feeling disappointed. He was probably getting sick of carrying her around like an invalid.

"Of course I can. Take your time." She made her way slowly toward the door, the hairs at the back of her neck prickling. Uneasy, she looked back over her shoulder. He was gone. She hurried up the front steps, wondering what he could possibly need out of the garage. Hopefully not big garbage bags and a shovel. She giggled at her own paranoia, nearly ramming her toes into a large flowerpot beside the door as she reached for the handle.

"Careful."

The single word murmured low in her ear sent adrenaline racing down her spine. Her muscles tensed and she froze, fearing the worst. His breath moved hot across her collarbone as the blood pounded in her ears.

A phone started ringing behind the door. Startled,

Claire jerked to the side, tripping over the flowerpot.

* * *

"Whoa, there." Adam caught her just before she crashed into the iron railing, pulling her up tight to his body.

"Are you okay?" He took a small step back, his hands on her waist as he turned her to look at him. Her pale face and glassy eyes told him everything he needed to know.

"Come on - let's get you set up in the guest room. You need rest. And painkillers."

She flinched as he leaned around her to shove the door open. Moving back, he held one hand out, gesturing for her to go first. She stepped over the threshold sideways, keeping him in view as he followed her into the entryway. The phone stopped ringing.

"Why did you sneak up behind me?" Her voice was raspy, with a note of fear in it. He shut the door and locked it, turning back to see her shoulders tensed. If he didn't know better, he'd think she was preparing for a fight.

"I wasn't sneaking." He stepped around her and went into the living room. "Come here, there's someone I want you to meet." He flipped on the light switch, glancing back over his shoulder. She was standing where he'd left her, just staring at him.

"What's wrong, Claire? Are you okay?" A beep signaled a message on his answering machine. He wondered who would be calling so late.

She slowly shook her head. "I thought you were getting something out of the garage. Where is it?" She took a step back towards the door.

"Just out back - I was going to go get him. Just stay there, okay? I'll be right back." He walked across the living room, hoping she wouldn't run as he continued through the kitchen and opened the back door. A large black shape bounded past his legs, claws scrabbling on the linoleum floor as it raced for the living room. Adam closed and locked the door before he followed, grinning as he imagined the look on Claire's face when Sly introduced himself. His dog might be energetic, but he couldn't be accused of having bad manners.

The first thing he saw when he came around the corner was Sly, sitting politely with one paw raised as his tail swished back and forth over the floor. Surprised that Claire wasn't fawning over him like most people, he looked up and saw her standing perfectly still, her back pressed tightly against the door.

"Claire?"

"You have a dog." Her stare moved from the dog to him, and back to the dog. "Why didn't you tell me you have a dog? Call him off!"

He frowned. "He's not attacking you. He's just saying hi." He walked around to shake Sly's paw, then scratched the dog behind his ears. "See? He's friendly."

"He only *looks* friendly. If I move, he'll come after me."

Adam put his palm out flat in front of Sly's nose to signal the dog to stay, then walked over to Claire.

"No, he won't. Not unless I tell him to, anyway." He reached out and took her hand, pulling her gently away from the door. "Have you always been afraid of dogs?"

"Not small ones," she said, never taking her eyes off Sly. "I got bit by the neighbor's dog in grade school - it was a black fuzzy dog with a black tongue." She frowned at Sly, squinting. "Not the same type as yours, I don't think." The dog thumped his tail on the floor. Adam led her past Sly into the living room.

"You're right," he said, motioning for her to sit on the couch. "Sly's a German Shepherd. The one that bit you was probably a chow. They can be extremely protective of their property." He looked over at Sly and chuckled. The dog was still sitting in the same spot, his head twisted over his shoulder as he strained to see what was going on in the living room.

"Come on, Sly." he said, earning a frightened look from Claire.

"Don't bring him over here!" She pushed herself into the corner of his plush couch, drawing both knees up and wrapping her arms around them. "Ow!" She glared at him, adjusting her foot to take pressure off her toes.

Sly came running, sitting in front of Adam to lift a paw again. Adam shook it, then pointed to a large stuffed pillow across the room.

"Go lay down for awhile. Good boy." The dog trotted off to his bed. "He's well trained - you don't have to worry about him bothering you. If you decide you want to pet him, just call him over. He'll be nice."

Claire nodded, but he could still see the fear in her eyes. If anyone could get her to come around, it was Sly, but the dog wouldn't push.

He walked around the couch to the long table on the other side, and pressed a button on his answering machine. Heavy breathing came through the speaker, and then a muffled, unfamiliar voice.

"Tell your new girlfriend to forget about running for mayor if she knows what's good for her." Claire gasped as Adam came back to the couch and sat down.

"This is all wrong." He ran a hand through his hair, scowling at the coffee table. "No one should even know that you and I were together tonight. Whoever that was," he pointed over his shoulder, "must have been watching us."

* * *

"I'm dropping out of the race." Claire stared at her toes. "I was going to anyway - there's no way I can campaign effectively with my toes broken and Stacy is acting weird. Now with this..." she glanced over at her would-be bodyguard and shrugged. "It just seems smarter to drop out."

He leaned forward, resting his elbows on his knees. "You don't have to do that. We'll call the police and report this guy - it won't be a problem. Most of the time it's just the opposing candidate anyway, trying to scare the competition. It happened to my dad all the time."

"We're not calling the police." She met his gaze and he raised his eyebrows. "They won't do anything anyway. Or they never did when..." She paused, resting her chin on her knees before she continued. "Whenever we got threats from one of Mom's boyfriends, the answer was always the same. They can't do anything unless something actually happens - something physical. Threats don't count."

He reached out and ran a finger across her tattoo, sending a shiver of awareness through her ankle. "What about this? Are you sure you want to give up your dream, just like that? If you don't even try, he wins."

"I don't know what else to do." She yawned, blinking back tears again. Embarrassed, she looked away, catching a glimpse of Sly sleeping on his bed. He looked so cozy, all curled up in a fur ball, and she yawned again.

"I'm just so tired, and I can't think..." The cushions moved as Adam slid closer, and his long arm curving gently around her shoulders. Against her better judgment, she leaned into his warmth, taking care to keep her toes pointed away from his hard thigh. His fingers brushed her chin, and when she turned her head back to him, his lips lightly brushed hers.

It was only the barest touch, but she craved more. His breath was hot on her skin as she looked up into his eyes, and she leaned in to gently nuzzle her mouth against his chin. Then he kissed her again, for real this time and her head swirled in a sensual fog. His tongue waged a tender assault that she met with her own, the taste of him only fueling her need for more. A whimper escaped her throat as he deepened the kiss, sending a rush of heat through her body to pool in her core.

He pulled back, and then dipped down for one more kiss before slowly pulling farther away.

"I...um..." His voice rasped and Claire frowned as the coolness slid back over his eyes. She tried to shake off the desire he'd ignited to no avail. He tried again. "We probably shouldn't be doing this." He stood, pacing in front of her, the only evidence of his arousal just moments ago the huge bulge in his jeans right at eye level. Her fingers itched to free him. To touch.

"Why not?" She gave him a small smile, until the doubt crowded in. Maybe he hadn't felt the overwhelming connection that she had. She felt sick at the thought and her smile faded.

He ran his hand through his hair. He did that a lot, not that she minded. It gave him a slightly rumpled, sexy appearance.

"Because you're tired - we're tired. And we need to talk. The campaign, the stalker, that tattoo with the same initials as mine..."

Claire sat back as if she'd been hit. "You'd rather talk about my tattoo than take me to bed?"

* * *

The minute the words were out of her mouth, Claire wished she could take them back. Adam stopped pacing, and sat on the coffee table in front of her. He didn't look at her, just reached out to run his finger over her tattoo again.

"Why do you keep doing that?" She wished he would look up. She wanted to see his eyes, to study the lines of his face.

His fingers moved slowly, methodically around her ankle, then a little higher to massage her calf.

"I've always loved the feel of bare skin," he said, moving his hand closer to her knee. "Tell me about the tattoo, Claire. Whose initials are those? Who stole your heart so long ago, and never gave it back?"

"It doesn't matter." She scooted away from his touch, carefully getting up off the couch. "I'm tired, and I don't feel like playing games. Do you have a guest room, or am I sleeping on the couch?"

She moved away, the need to put distance between them almost overwhelming. A shuffling noise from the far wall drew her attention and she fought the urge to run. Adam's dog sat up on his bed, ears alert and head cocked to the side as if he was just waiting for her to move.

"On second thought, if you don't have a guest room, point me to your room and you can have the couch. I'm not sleeping without a door between your dog and me."

Adam stepped over the table in a smooth motion, swinging her up in to his arms. Again.

"We'll talk about this in the morning," he said gruffly, pausing only to flip the light off before he carried her down the hall and through an open door to the left. Three seconds later she was sinking into a thick quilt, her protest cut off when his mouth covered hers in a punishing kiss. His muscles were taut with restraint as he settled over her on the bed and she couldn't make herself push him away. So many years she'd longed for this - for him. He trailed kisses down the side of her neck and across her collarbone. Long fingers skated along her neckline, pushing the wrap-style top aside. Hot breath caressed the delicate skin and she tugged on his shoulder, urging him to take what he wanted.

His lips grazed her breast, a shiver of pleasure shooting to her core as she arched up, silently begging for more. One of his hands slid down her ribcage to smooth over her hip.

And then he stopped, pushing up off the bed with a growl.

Claire barely suppressed a cry of frustration as she tried to shake off the sensual fog. Grateful for the darkness she sat up, pulling her dress together as a different kind of heat rose in her face. She tried to find words, but ended up just staring as he paced back and forth beside the bed.

"I'm sorry," he said, his voice thick and raspy. He ran a hand through his hair, turning toward her, but looking at the floor. "I shouldn't have done that. It's late, we're tired, and there are things that should be cleared up before we--"

Claire nearly laughed, if only to keep from crying. "I don't believe it," she said, shaking her head. "You're turning me down because you're tired? Or because you want to talk? Either way, what kind of a guy does that? I know I'm not exactly in top form to-night, but damn."

"That's not fair." He bent over enough to look her in the eye. "You know I'm attracted to you." Even in the dark, she could see the sincerity and con-fusion in his gaze. "I'm not interested in using you, Claire. Haven't you figured that out yet?"

She shrugged. "Then what do you want?"

He caressed the side of her face. "I want what I was too stupid and scared to go after in high school. But I don't want to rush it. I want to do it right."

"What does that mean, exactly?" Her heart pounded as she waited, not realizing just how badly she wanted to hear him say it.

"It..." he frowned as a loud bark, then another came from another part of the house. Straightening up, he looked toward the door. "Something's wrong – that's a warning bark." He glanced over his shoulder at her, his expression grim. "Stay here. I'll be right back." He strode to the door, closing it behind him and she let the breath she hadn't realized she was holding out. Of course the man would just walk out in the middle of the most important conversation of her entire life.

She swung her legs off the edge of the bed and rubbing her face in her hands. Inhaling deeply, she frowned. Was that smoke?

Suddenly she realized that the fog wasn't all in her head and she recognized a frantic note in the now-constant barking. She stood, wincing only slightly as a rush of energy sent her running out into the hall.

"Adam? Adam where are you?" The smoke got thicker as she moved down the hall, and she dropped to her knees, searching for breathable air. Coughing, she stopped, propping herself up against the wall and pulling the neck of her shirt up over her mouth. Through watery eyes she squinted through the smoke then turned to look the other way. Sweat ran down the sides of her face as intense heat seemed to engulf her and she knew she had to get out of there, fast.

Chapter Three

Looking the other way again, she remembered seeing a window at the opposite end of the hall. But the dog had been in the living room. Adam would have gone that way, for sure. She started crawling toward the front door, determined not to leave him behind.

A raspy bark made her freeze, and she glanced back over her shoulder to see Adam's dog staring at her. His head was lowered and he barked again, wheezing a few times before he turned and took a few steps in the opposite direction. Did he want her to follow him?

The dog barked again then coughed, his tail low and nearly between his legs. He was obviously suffering. Sure that Adam would want her to save his dog; she turned and crawled the other way, the dog staying a few steps ahead. Through the smoke she saw a dark mass on the floor ahead and as she got closer, Claire gasped, coughing as more smoke burned her lungs.

"Adam!" She hurried to his side, panic rising as she saw the blood pooling beneath his head. Had he fallen? His dog whined, pacing between the end of the hall and his master's body. Was he dead, she wondered? She slid two fingers onto his neck, searching for a pulse. Nothing. The smoke was thickening. She couldn't do anything for him until they got outside.

Forcing herself up she spotted a fake plant in the corner, and hoped the pot wasn't plastic. Quickly she stepped over Adam and picked up the heavy porcelain pot, throwing it as hard as she could into the window. The glass shattered out and she knocked the remaining shards out of the lower and side frames with her elbow. Fresh, cool air streamed in, sending the thick smoke billowing out into the night.

She took several deep breaths of clean air, imagining she could feel it replacing the smoke in her lungs. Suddenly she was very aware of the severe pain in her foot and it was all she could do to keep from dropping to the ground and grabbing her toes.

Instead she patted the windowsill, pleased when the dog still had the energy to vault over it. She glanced out to make sure he was okay, then hurried back to Adam's side.

Reaching under his armpits, she dragged him to lay right in front of the window. Peering out again, she judged the distance to the ground. There was no way to lower him down gently and they were out of time. Flames were licking at the hallway as she leaned over him and pulled his right arm up onto the windowsill, then his right leg. Shoving at his hips, she managed to get his left toe out, and then suddenly gravity took over and his body was slipping neatly through the window.

She grabbed for his hands, surprised when his fingers locked around her wrists. It took all of her strength to lower him until his feet touched the ground. Then she let go, watching him crumple into a heap below. She crawled out after him. In the brief flash she was conscious as her feet touched the ground, she remembered her two broken toes.

* * *

A rhythmic whooshing sound coupled with the faint stench of antiseptic coaxed Adam back to consciousness. He blinked, trying to make out the unfamiliar shapes that seemed to loom over him through a blurry fog. He started to raise a hand and then stopped, wincing at an uncomfortable pull at the back of his hand. The back of his head felt like it was on fire, and he couldn't hold back a low moan at the pain. What the hell had happened to him?

"Adam?"

He knew that voice. "Claire?" He turned toward

the sound, wincing again as a zing of pain shot through his skull. "What happened? Are you okay?" Carefully he opened his eyes again, trying to focus on her face in the dim light.

"Your house was on fire, and you were bleeding..." She took a breath, squeezing his hand briefly. "I had to drop you out of a window."

He closed his eyes, carefully swallowing. His mouth was dry.

"Water?" he managed, his tongue too thick. He heard her shuffle around the room as the memory of those last moments before losing consciousness started to come back. A moment of panic hit suddenly.

"Sly - is he okay?" He forced the words out, gratefully accepting the straw she pressed between his lips.

"He'll be fine." She smiled, pulling the cup away too soon. "The firefighters gave him oxygen, and the vet wanted to keep him overnight just to be sure." She set the cup down, and took his hand again. "He saved us, you know. He led me right to you."

Adam nodded and closed his eyes. He was so tired.

The next time he woke, he was alone. The lights were too bright, and he shielded his face with one hand as he looked around, wondering where Claire had gone. Or had he only dreamed she was there?

The door opened, and she walked in. It took a moment for him to notice the damp redness on her cheeks, and he frowned as she walked by him to reach for the purse in a nearby recliner.

"What's wrong?" he asked, annoyed at how weak he sounded. She stepped over to the bed, leaning down to peck his cheek with her cold lips.

"Your family is here," she said, flinching as the door opened behind her. "I have to go."

"No wait - stay!" Satisfied that the words sounded stronger than the last, he looked up as his mother, brother and father filed into the room. Claire hesitated, clearly weighing her options. Taking a breath, she returned to his side and he reached for her hand.

His mother clicked over to the bed in her high heels.

"Don't be silly, dear," she said, pushing her way past Claire to give him a kiss on the cheek. "We're here now, there's no need to make the poor girl stay. I'm sure she has something she needs to get back to. Can I get you some water?"

He looked around her to where Claire had been standing, but she wasn't there. She wasn't anywhere else either and he glared up at his mom.

"What did you tell her? Why did you send her away? Get her back. I want her here."

"Now darling--"

"No mother. If anyone's leaving, it's you." He pressed a button to raise the head of his bed. "What are you doing here anyway? Don't you have a campaign to run?" He looked at David, wondering if he knew that their mother had just sent his running mate away. Probably not, since Claire hadn't had time to announce her campaign yet.

Leona stepped back, a hand to her heart in mock surprise. "Don't tell me you have a 'thing' for Claire Taylor. She may have grown up, but she's still trailer-trash, son. You need to focus on getting well and feeling better."

Adam saw the spikes come faster on his heart monitor as he silently fumed. He pressed the call button, needing someone, anyone, to rescue him from his own flesh and blood.

Just as he was getting ready to plead his case to his father, the door swung open again.

"Adam, where's Claire? Are you o--" Stacy burst into the room and looked up from her phone, stopping short as her gaze landed on David where he stood leaning against the wall. Adam nearly winced at the almost palpable tension coming from their general direction.

"I'm okay," Adam said, drawing her attention away from his brother. "You just missed Claire. She was...upset." He glared at his mother. "I think she's--"

"You never called me back," David broke in, pushing away from the wall. Adam frowned, trying to remember the last message he'd gotten. His brother's eyes were on Stacy though, and judging from the way she was gripping her phone it had struck the intended nerve.

She shook her head, taking a step backward. "I

don't have time for this, David. This isn't the time or place." She pivoted, turning her back on him. Adam finally noticed she was wearing the same suit from last night. Strands of her hair were sticking out in odd directions and she swayed a little, catching herself with a firm hand on the end of his bed.

"We have to stop her," she said as her phone started to buzz. "We can't let her go through with the campaign. It's too dangerous." She pushed a button on her phone and stared at the screen.

Adam looked over at his mother, still standing beside the bed. Her neutral expression betrayed nothing and for a moment he considered asking if she'd been at the hotel last night with Stacy. The mattress shifted at his feet and he looked back to see Stacy perched carefully on the edge. Sweat beaded her forehead, and she reached up to rub her neck as she fingered more keys on her phone.

"Hey - don't worry. Last night Claire was pretty sure she was going to back out anyway. I'm sure she just went home." He tried to lean forward, pain shooting through the back of his head again. Feeling helpless and annoyed, he barked at David.

"Go find a doctor - something's wrong with her."

Stacy wiped her forehead again, her breath coming in short gasps. "We're too late," she breathed, dropping the phone on the bed. "She's at the press conference now."

Adam found a remote control clipped to his mattress. He pointed it at the TV and turned it on. "What channel?"

"F--Five."

Adam found the right channel as he pressed frantically on his call button with the other. Stacy was lying across his feet now and he scowled at his parents, neither of them moving.

"Isn't someone going to help her?" Thank god he could still feel her breathing, but it seemed too slow. Panicking, he pushed himself up, gritting his teeth at the pain and leaning over to shake her shoulders. "Stacy? Stacy!"

The door swung open and David rushed in, two nurses behind him. "Over there." He pointed, and the women moved quickly to the bed, one of them pushing Adam back.

"Everyone out of the room," the other one said, her voice calm but firm as she felt Stacy's neck for a pulse. The room filled up fast as a doctor strode quickly through the door, followed by another man in scrubs pushing a bed. The second nurse ushered Adam's family out the door as the two men put Stacy on the gurney and rolled her away. One nurse stayed behind and as she bustled around adjusting his bedding and monitors, he looked up at the screen again.

Claire was at the podium, a smile that didn't quite pass for real on her lips. He turned up the sound as the camera zoomed in, the close-up image accentuating the weariness in her eyes. The nurse tried to push him back down onto the pillow, but he shook his head, numb to the pain.

"Someone has been threatening me," she began, her low tone forcing the murmuring down so people could hear. "Someone wants to make sure that I don't run for the office of Mayor." A rumble went through the crowd of reporters, flashes going off from every direction as she held her hands up, asking for silence.

"There are a lot of people who don't want to see a girl like me, who grew up poor on the wrong side of town, sitting in that office. But I have news for all of you. You can't scare me away. I've worked long and hard to pull myself up out of that life, and I think the people of this town need someone like me to bring a new perspective and a fresh voice to the Mayor's office." Her voice had grown stronger, and with every word, she seemed to stand taller, straighter.

"That's my girl," Adam whispered as she continued.

"My name is Claire Taylor. And I want to be your next Mayor."

* * *

Claire walked away from the podium as her announcement triggered a low rumble throughout the meeting room. She'd taken a few questions, but Stacy still hadn't shown up and the questions were turning more personal. Promising another conference later and personal interviews set up through her campaign office, she'd ended the session. Once she moved out of sight, she slumped against the wall and kicked off the low heels that were killing her mangled toes. Her thoughts drifted back to the hospital, and her conversation with Adam's mother in the hall.

Leona Cranston had made it clear that she'd do anything to ensure Adam's brother David got elected mayor. The woman had implied she wouldn't flinch at making things up, if need be, or bringing Claire's mother into the spotlight, and considering everything that had happened already, Claire couldn't help but wonder if that included setting fire to her son's house. But Leona had seemed genuinely surprised about the incident, so either she was a really good actress, or someone else had been behind the fire.

Claire had been ready to end the campaign after their little talk – it wasn't worth all the danger, not only to her, but to the people around her. Then she'd gone into Adam's room to get her things. He wanted her to stay with him, even in the face of his mother's clear dismissal. He believed in her. That had helped her remember why she was running for office in the first place.

"Ms. Taylor?"

Claire looked up at her name, her pulse speeding up as a young man in a suit strode toward her. Sliding her feet back into her shoes, she tried not to wince as her toes protested the bondage.

"Yes?" She remembered to smile and hold out her hand as he reached her. "What can I do for you?"

He gripped her hand for only a second, his shoulders tense. "I have a message for you," he said, holding out a folded piece of paper. As soon as she took it, he walked away, as if he resented the errand.

Her hands shaking, she unfolded the paper and stared at the note. Shivers rolled down her spine at the two neatly printed words.

You're next.

Next for what she could only guess, but considering the fire at Adam's house and her chat with his mother, it seemed like anything was possible.

She crumpled the paper and tossed it into a nearby trash can, then walked down the hall and out to her car in the back lot. She'd go home, get a shower and make sure everything was okay, then go back to the hospital to check on Adam. This time Leona would just have to step aside.

Ten minutes later, she pulled into her driveway. She took the keys out of the ignition but before she could get out the phone rang. Reaching for the door latch she pushed it open, holding the phone with her other hand.

"Hello?"

"Claire," Adam's voice made her pause, even as her heart sped up. "Where are you right now?'

She let go of the handle, giving him her full attention. "Sitting in my driveway. I was about to go take a shower and come see you, actually. How are you feeling?"

"I'm fine," he said, a hard edge to his voice that left her cold. "Listen to me - you need to get out of there right now. Don't go inside. Just come back to the hospital."

Claire frowned, peering at her little house through the windshield. A cottage, really, the outside was all done in red brick, with dark brown wood trim around the windows and doors. Crocus were blooming in the flowerbeds out front, and she could see the dim light from the lamp she always left on shining through the front window, just as she'd left it.

"But everything looks fine," she said shrugging her shoulders even though he couldn't see the gesture. "Can't I just grab some clean clothes?"

Claire could nearly taste Adam's frustration through the phone. "No. Someone tried to poison Stacy today, and considering the fire at my house, who knows what could be rigged at your place. I have a really bad feeling about this. Get away from that place as fast as you can. Please."

"Stacy? Is she okay?" The car door was ajar and Claire swung it out a little so she could close it firmly. Switching the phone to her left ear, she turned the key.

"She will be. Are you leaving?"

"I'm leaving now," she said, shifting into reverse and backing out of the driveway. "I'll be there in ten minutes."

"Good." Adam paused, and she wondered if he'd hung up. "I'll see you when--"

The phone flew out of Claire's hand and the car bucked as roaring thunder vibrated through her body. She squeezed her eyes shut, instinctively covering her head with her arms while a series of thuds traveled across the roof. A brief hailstorm followed, and then finally, silence. She opened her eyes and slowly straightened in her seat to see a thick cloud of dust in every direction.

"Claire? Claire! Are you okay?" Adam's voice drifted from somewhere on the other side of the car, and she finally spotted her phone on the floor. Hands shaking, she leaned over to pick it up, dropping it once before she pressed it to her ear.

"I--I'm here," she said, hearing the words as if she were speaking into a tunnel. "I think something blew up!" She twisted, trying to peer through the soupy white fog. "I can't see anything...the dust is so thick."

"Claire, listen to me. Can you drive?"

She shook her head, trying to hold back the panic rising in her chest. "I can't see, and it's so hot in here. I need to get out--"

"No!" He yelled in her ear, jolting her out of her shock for the moment. "Don't open the door. I know it's hot, but you'll be safer in the car. Just start the engine and go slow. The dust should dissipate soon."

She took a deep breath, put the phone down on

the passenger seat and turned the key, thankful when
the engine purred back to life. Her chest tight with
too-thick air, she pressed down on the gas, easing forward a few inches at a time. The dust started to thin,
and gradually familiar objects began to take shape
around her. At the corner, she stopped and looked
over her shoulder at the house-shaped shadows that
made up her block. They were all there except one.
Her little cottage had disappeared completely.

She picked up the phone, swiping at a tear on her
cheek.

"My house is gone," she said, her mind numb. "I
don't have anywhere to go." She turned the corner,
not sure where she was going, but needing to go
somewhere. "My house..."

"Shhh...it's okay." The soft, deep tone was calm-
ing to her soul. "Come to the hospital, up to my
room. We'll figure it out."

Claire nodded and then snapped the phone shut,
tossing it on the other seat again. She realized she'd
been heading towards the hospital all along. She focused on the street, on the traffic lights and signs.
Anything to keep her mind off of her house explod-
ing. If Adam hadn't called, hadn't told her to leave
right away...

She parked in the lot and got out, not bothering
to lock the door behind her. If they wanted the car
too, they could have it. Walking through the sterile
white halls she felt like she was in a dream, waiting for

the nightmare to continue.

The nurse's station was vacant as she passed by. Just as well, so she wouldn't have to justify her presence again. Adam's room was around the corner on the right and her feet grew heavy as she got closer, wondering if his family was still there. Was she up to facing his mother again so soon?

The back of her neck tingled as she passed the last room before his and she stopped, her heart suddenly pounding. A sharp prick in her shoulder was the last thing she felt before everything faded to black.

Chapter Four

Stacy opened her eyes, a white tiled ceiling coming slowly into focus as a wave of nausea rolled through her stomach. She coughed, barely holding back the dry heaves that followed. A low moan escaped as she twisted to her side on the bed, pulling her knees up to try to stop the queasiness. What was happening to her?

"Easy there…breathe. Here's some water."

David.

She blinked back the moisture blurring her vision, focusing on breathing. In and out. David approached the bed, his intimidating black suit negated only a little by the pink plastic cup in one hand. He held the straw to her lips and she took a few tentative sips. Better.

"Thank you," she said, her voice raspy. "What are you doing here? What happened?"

He set the cup down and tilted his head to stare at her for a long moment. "You collapsed at my brother's feet. The doctor said it was some kind of poison. They gave you something to counteract it, but it was touch and go for awhile there. The worst of it is over - you should be okay in a day or so."

Her eyelids felt heavy, and she let them drift shut until his words fully sank in. "Claire," she croaked, forcing her eyes to open once more. "I have to talk to her, convince her to--"

"Shhh...just rest. There's nothing you can do right now." He came closer, smoothing a hand over her shoulder only to draw back when she flinched at his touch. "Why didn't you call?"

She searched his face for any trace of judgment, but found none. Letting out a deep sigh, she closed her eyes again.

"It didn't work the first time, David. It wasn't going to work the second, especially with your mother in the picture. I thought it would just be easier to stop it before it got started again."

"So if that wasn't a new start, what was it? Pity sex?" His footsteps moved away and in her mind she could see him instinctively running a hand through that feathery brown hair. Even in grade school he'd always done that when faced with something stressful. She knew she should reassure him, try to explain. But it was better this way. Safer for him.

"Will you bring me my phone? I need to call

Claire. It's really important that I talk to her. She can't continue with the race. She has to drop out."

He shook his head, striding across the room to a small dresser. He dug around in her purse for a moment before holding up her phone.

"Like I said - there's nothing you can do. She announced her candidacy just a few minutes after you collapsed." He handed her the device and she punched in Claire's number, praying her friend would pick up the phone. David frowned, moving toward the door. She wondered if he was finally leaving. The call was transferred to Claire's voice mail.

"Claire? It's Stacy. Look, I'm sorry for all the trouble I've caused but you're in danger. Someone might actually try to kill you. So call me as soon as you get this message, okay?" She disconnected the call, watching as David peered out the window into the hall. "What is it - what's out there?"

He pulled the door open. "Dial her number again."

Stacy pushed number five, Claire's number on speed-dial. Almost immediately a song started playing out in the hall. She let it ring several times, each one followed by the looped ring tone. Confused, she watched David go out into the hall and pick something up off the floor. He returned holding the phone up in one hand and a familiar key ring in the other.

"Is this Claire's phone? And are these her keys?"

* * *

Claire woke with a start, instinctively turning her head as the strong smell of ammonia burned in her nose. She tried to roll onto her side, but tight straps at her shoulders, hips and thighs held her prone. Something smelled musty. The low hum of machinery and the bright light overhead assaulted her senses and she moved her head from side to side, desperate to escape the chaos. Beyond the cone of light, all was dark. Her pulse was racing and she strained against the restraints that held her wrists and ankles immobile.

"Help!" She blinked at the tears forming in her eyes. "Help me, please!"

"No one can hear you." A low chuckle came from somewhere above her head. She tilted her head back as far as she could, peering into the darkness. "Come on, Claire. You know how this works. If you see my face, I can't let you go. Ever."

She let her shoulders fall back to the table and tried to slow her breathing. Where had she heard that voice before?

"So you're not going to kill me?"

"Not if you do as I say." He had moved to the right. Claire fought the urge to glance over. "We have some things to discuss. Like your candidacy for mayor."

She swallowed hard. "What do you want me to do?"

He tapped the table near her ankle. "You were supposed to change your mind and not run for mayor. You've already ruined that. It would look suspicious if you pulled out this late. So what I want from you…" warm fingers slid up the side of her bare foot, then pinched her broken toes. Claire cried out, arching up against her bonds until he removed the pressure.

"I want you to lose, Claire. Throw the race." He squeezed her toes again, sending a jolt of pain up through her leg and into her hip.

"And if I don't?" She gasped as he let go of her toes, running his finger down over the tattoo on her ankle.

"Then you die."

A needle slid into her thigh, and suddenly she was very tired. She tried to stop her head from falling sideways, but it was just too heavy. Her eyes closed as if someone had shut them for her. As the world drifted away again, she thought she heard laughter in the background.

* * *

Adam checked the clock on the wall, absently fingering the plastic band at his wrist. Claire should have made it by now. Something must have happened. He pushed the call button. Maybe she'd gone to visit Stacy first. Had he told her about the poisoning? He rubbed the back of his neck, wishing his head didn't hurt so badly.

"Is Claire here?" David pushed through the door, scanning the room before finally looking at the bed. "I found these in the hall outside Stacy's room..." He placed a phone and a set of keys in Adam's hand just as a nurse came striding in.

Adam shook his head, staring down at the phone. "She was supposed to meet me here over twenty minutes ago. I was just going to ask the nurse if she went to see Stacy." He looked up at his brother, panic rising in his chest. "Something happened to her. We have to find her."

"I'll go check with the nurse's station and see if we can organize a search. She can't have gotten far, not in so little time." David squeezed Adam's shoulder once then turned away. "We'll find her. I'm sure she's okay. I need to go tell Stacy what's up, but I'll be back."

Adam sat for another minute before he took the monitor off his finger. He pulled the IV needle free and swung his legs off the bed, the room swirling around him. When it stopped, he eased off the bed and moved carefully to the small wardrobe on the other side of the room. With any luck, his clothes would be there.

Five minutes later he was dressed. The door opened and the nurse came in, scowling when she spotted him. "What are you doing out of bed?"

"A friend is missing, somewhere in or around the hospital. I have to find her. She could be hurt."

The nurse shook her head. "We have people look-ing for her," she said, straightening the covers on his bed. "You aren't going to be any help in your present condition though, so you just crawl right back into this bed and rest. If your friend is here, the security team will find her. I'll keep you informed but for now--"

Adam walked to the window and stared out at the rooftops surrounding the hospital. Was she out there, he wondered? He turned, determined to help with the search even if he had to muscle his way past the nurse. A flutter of movement caught his eye from be-low, and he turned back, peering down into the court-yard below.

"Mr. Cranston, I have to insist--"

"That's Claire!" He motioned for her to join him then pointed to the manicured lawn below. "That's her, sitting up on that bed down there. How do we get there? I have to go to her..."

The nurse ran for the door. "You stay here," she called over her shoulder. "I'll get someone out there."

Adam was almost to the door when David came in. "I heard a nurse out there say something about a girl in the courtyard. Did they find Claire?"

"Go look out that window," Adam said, pointing. He followed David, making it to the bed where he sat to rest. "I was just going to go down there. Do you know which way the stairwell is?" He wiped his brow with the back of his hand, surprised when it came away damp. Why was it so hot in his room?

David turned back, his brows drawn together. "You're not going to be any use to Claire in your condition. I'll make sure she's taken care of. Call Stacy for me, and tell her Claire's okay."

Adam nodded, swinging his feet awkwardly back onto the bed. "What's Stacy's room number?"

"Three-five-two-zero. I'll be back as soon as I can." He left, and Adam reached for the phone.

* * *

A soft breeze wafted across Claire's cheek, coaxing her back to consciousness. She opened her eyes to fluffy white clouds floating overhead and smiled, realizing it all must have been a horrible dream. Glancing at her surroundings, she wondered where she'd fallen asleep. A park, maybe? She swung her legs over the side of the bed, flinching as the back of her calves hit cold metal.

Sitting up, she examined her attire. A paper-thin hospital gown barely covered her nakedness and she hugged her arms over her chest, her breathing coming faster. It wasn't a dream.

Behind her, the sound of something metal hitting stone sent her sliding off the edge of the gurney, a small whimper escaping her lips as her knees buckled under the unwanted weight. Footsteps pounded closer and she tried to crawl behind the nearby bushes, but she was too weak. With time running out, she grabbed a sizable stick.

And then he was there, standing in front of her.

"Miss, are you okay?"

She swung the stick hard at his legs, catching him mid-knee from behind. He gave a yelp and went down hard, landing on his backside right in front of her before his words finally registered in her brain. She scooted farther away, tossing the stick aside.

"Who are you? What do you want?

He held up one hand, taking a few deep breaths before answering. "I work here. You're Claire Taylor, right? I'm here to help you."

Rusty hinges squeaked behind her and she winced, rubbing her forehead with one hand. "How do I know? How can I trust--" A long shadow loomed over her as another person approached.

"Claire, thank God. It's David. Are you okay?"

She looked up, but couldn't see his face. "David?" Shielding her eyes from the sunlight, she could just barely make out his features. "Where's Adam? I was going to see Adam..."

He held out a hand to her. "He's in his room. I'll take you to him. Are you sure you're okay?"

She shook her head, tears coming to the surface. "I'm so tired...and my legs don't seem to work. I don't understand..."

"It's okay." He leaned down so she could look at his face. "I'll carry you. Are you ready?"

She nodded, forcing herself to lift her arms to his neck as he scooped her up in his arms, making sure the hospital gown was secured around her. He carried her inside, where three nurses and a doctor were waiting.

"We'll put her in room eleven-oh-four for now, just there to your right." One of the nurses pointed to a doorway across the hall, and Claire shook her head, struggling to get free.

"No! I need to see Adam - where is he?"

David held her tighter, passing the assigned room and heading straight for the elevator.

"We're going to him now," he said as the doors slid open. "Just hang on." Claire tightened her hold around his neck, her heart racing in fear.

"Sir, sir...you can't..." One of the nurses caught the doors as they started to close, stepping into the opening. "We need to do an exam. You can't take her anywhere until we release her."

Claire raised her head, looking straight at the woman. "He didn't hurt me," she said, glancing down at the faux wood floor. "You can come with me, see for yourself."

The nurse sighed, and stepped onto the elevator. When they reached Adam's floor, Claire patted David's shoulder to get his attention.

"I think I can walk now," she pushed against this

chest and he set her down, keeping a steadying arm around her waist until he know she could walk. Making her way slowly down the hall, she pushed the door to Adam's room open and took several steps in before he noticed she was there.

She hurried to sit on the bed beside him and laid her head on his chest, relieved when his arms encircled her in a giant hug.

"I'm so glad you're safe," he said, pushing her out a little to look in her eyes. "You're really okay? Did the doctor check you out?"

She smiled, barely able to keep her eyes open. She was so very tired.

"David got me past the doctor. I just wanted to see you. Some psycho kidnapped me." Her smile faded, and she sat up, her hands slipping over his chest. The motion sent a throb of aching pain through her right wrist, and she turned it over, gasping at the image that had been embedded in her skin.

Claire winced as Adam leaned forward, gently tugging at her fingers until she turned her wrist up for him to see. Angry red flesh surrounded three black links of a chain tattooed just below the palm of her hand.

"This is fresh," he said, peering closely at the image. "Not even an hour old, I'd guess."

The nurse came up beside them, looked at the wound and shook her head. "I'll get something to put on that for you. You really should lay down..."

"She's not leaving." His tone left no room for argument, and Claire looked up into his steely eyes, shivering at the intensity there.

The nurse looked at them for a long moment, then turned to leave. "I'll have them bring an extra bed in too." Her footsteps faded into the hall, and Claire looked down at the tattoo again. Behind her, David cleared his throat.

"If you're okay here, I need to go tell Stacy you're okay." She nodded, then turned, frowning up at him.

"How's she doing? Do they know who did it?"

He ran a hand through his hair, and sighed. "I'll let Adam fill you in. She's recovering. I'll bring her up in a little bit." She nodded and watched him leave before turning back to Adam with raised eyebrows.

"Stacy showed up just after you left, desperate to stop you from announcing your candidacy. She passed out right on my feet - literally. The doctors say she's very lucky she was in the hospital at the time, or they might not have been able to save her."

Claire felt sick to her stomach. "This is all my fault. I should have listened, should have just quit, maybe even moved--"

"That's crap." The blunt statement hit hard. "You had no way of knowing any of this would happen."

She shrugged, swiping at a tear. He was right, but that didn't make her feel any better. She'd thought she was ready for politics, but this...this was far worse than the advertising wars she'd envisioned. Why would anyone think it was so important for David to win instead of her? She didn't have any answers, only questions.

"What happened, Claire?" The soft question interrupted her thoughts, and she wondered how much she should tell him. "Do you remember anything?" Adam scooted over, patting the small space he'd managed to free beside him.

She lay on her side, snuggling up to his broad chest. Her foot started throbbing as she recalled the basement and warm, cruel fingers on her toes. The words spilled out. "He...he said I had to throw the race. And if I don't...he'll kill me."

"Just put it over here." Plastic rattled against metal as something large was wheeled into the room behind her.

A sharp pain shot through Claire's head at the nurse's command, and she carefully sat up to see what the commotion was. A second bed had been placed a few feet away near the wall and two orderlies bent over securing the wheels. The nurse went to a box on the wall and pulled out a pair of disposable gloves, pulling them over her fingers.

"Now, Miss - I need you to move over here please. The doctor will be in soon to check you over, and there are a couple of police officers outside who need to speak with you as soon as you're up to it. Do you need help standing?"

Claire shook her head, pushing to her feet and

walking cautiously over to the new bed. She sat on the edge and swung her legs up, every little movement punctuated by a sharp jab in her brain. Finally situated, she allowed the nurse to put some sort of salve on her new tattoo, the cool sensation a welcome relief.

A large male hand reached out to knock on the open door, and then a tall, black-haired cop moved into view.

"Ma'am, do you have a few minutes to answer some questions?"

Chapter Five

"I suppose," Claire said to the officer, wincing as the nurse started to pull a sheet and blanket up over her legs.

"Ow...my toes." She exhaled as the blankets were lifted off her feet and laid to the side. Following the nurse's gaze, she noticed that the slight greenish bruising had turned to an angry dark purple and one of her toes now sat at an impossibly twisted angle. Her stomach turned and her hands curled into the blanket, remembering how Adam had set them just the day before. She took deep breaths as she felt her pulse throbbing through her foot, causing a sharp burn that radiated up into her ankle.

"Those need to be set." The nurse turned and rolled off her gloves, tossing them neatly into the waste basket beside the bed. "I'll go get you something for the pain, and let the doctor know. He'll be awhile yet, so just relax if you can." Claire nodded as the woman walked out, past the cop still waiting in the doorway. His eyes were fixed on her toes, and his skin had gone pale.

She fought back a grin, the pain receding a little. Surely this tough guy had seen worse in his line of work. "Did you need to talk to me, officer?"

His gaze snapped up, as if he came out of a trance. "Um...yes. Officer Mumford, ma'am." He cleared his throat, paging through a small notebook as he took a couple more steps into the room. "Why don't you just start at the beginning, and tell me exactly what happened."

She glanced at Adam. He nodded towards Mumford, his eyebrows raised. She inhaled, then exhaled slowly, trying to decide what to do. The kidnapper hadn't told her to keep quiet, but what if it was implied? Could she take the risk?

"I don't remember much." She looked at down at her hands, then back up at the officer. "I was walking down the hall, coming to see Adam, and someone came up behind me and stuck something in my shoulder. Then everything went dark."

Mumford's pen scratched along the paper, the sound making Claire want to grit her teeth. "And when you woke up?"

"I was in the courtyard." She fought the urge to turn her head, feeling Adam's disappointment from across the room. Mumford stopped writing to stare at her, weariness evident in the lines around his eyes. He didn't say anything, and yet she felt pinned like a butterfly on display.

"I'm sorry," she said, dropping her gaze. "Maybe whatever he gave me screwed up my memory or something."

"How do you know your kidnapper was male?"

Claire shrugged. "I just assumed - I mean, aren't most of them? Do you think it could have been a woman?" She bit her bottom lip, looking up at him through her eyelashes without moving her head. It was another of her mom's old tricks, the innocent little girl, and she could tell by the tightening around his mouth that he wasn't buying it. She'd never been good at lying.

The nurse breezed back in and handed Claire a small paper cup with two pills inside. "These are going to make you a little drowsy," she said, handing over a cup of water. "But the doctor will be able to set your toes once they kick in."

Tossing back the pills she looked up at Officer Mumsford. "Do you mind if we finish this later? I'm tired, and if these make me sleepy..."

He stared at her for a long moment, assessing her with his eyes. "Just one more thing, Ms. Taylor." He paused until she raised her eyebrows. "Are you aware that your house blew up this afternoon?"

* * *

Adam felt sick as he watched Claire's eyes widen at the last question. She must have forgotten about the explosion in all the chaos, and the only thing stopping him from going to her side was the IV tugging at his hand. He cleared his throat, garnering Officer Mumsford's attention.

"Do you have any leads on who might have done it?" he asked, trying to redirect. It was obvious Claire wasn't ready to discuss it yet. Though he wasn't sure why she wanted to hide the previous threats.

Mumsford flipped through his notes. "Not yet. I was hoping Ms. Taylor could help fill in those blanks."

"I--I'm sorry." Claire shook her head. "I really don't know who--why anyone would want to kill me."

Adam tried again. "She's obviously in danger. Don't you think some sort of protection might be in order?" Claire's lips were trembling, moisture pooling in her eyes. Her skin was ghostly pale, and he wondered what was taking the doctor so long.

The officer looked at him for a long moment, assessing. Then he turned back to Claire. "I can assign you a temporary detail, but we're not in the habit of protecting every politician who gets threatened in the course of a campaign. So you'll have to hire your own security as soon as possible. Assuming you want it, that is."

She brushed away stray tears with a finger, glancing at Adam then quickly back at Mumsford. "I have a bodyguard," she said, her features smoothing into a calm facade. "But thank you."

"Can we have a few minutes, Sir?" Adam waited until Mumsford left, then looked over at Claire. She looked so lost, so helpless that his anger nearly dissipated.

"What were you thinking? Why didn't you tell him about everything - the threats, my house fire, your house, the basement." He shook his head, as if that would somehow make everything logical. "Why won't you let him help?"

She looked down at her hands, picking at the worn tan blanket. "I don't think I'm supposed to," she replied. The apathy in her weary voice scared him, and he slipped out of bed, careful to pull the IV stand with him as he made his way to her side. He tucked a stray piece of hair behind one of her ears, letting his fingers slide tenderly over her jawline until he could lift her chin.

"Don't give up," he said, gently forcing her to look in his eyes. "We'll beat this guy, I promise. But you should tell the police what you know. They have resources we don't." He released her chin, moving back a step.

"They can't protect me." She lay down on the bed, careful to keep her feet away from the blankets. She closed her eyes, her breathing slower. Adam couldn't resist tracing a finger down the side of her face.

"I can," he whispered, leaning over to brush her

cheek with his lips. He pulled the blanket up over her shoulders then went to his wardrobe, retrieving his cell phone from the top shelf. It was time to call in a couple of favors. He punched in a number and walked to the window, staring down into the court-yard as he waited for the call to connect.

* * *

Claire woke to hot, throbbing pain encasing her foot and ankle. She rolled over, tossing the hospital covers off in an attempt to relieve the pressure. Swinging her legs over the side of the bed she sat up, hissing under her breath as the blood flowed faster in her feet. As she slid off the bed, she looked at the tape around her toes, holding them together from top to bottom. It hadn't hurt as bad getting them set the second time, but that was probably the drugs. She glanced over at the second bed expecting to see Adam, but the bed was empty.

Moving slowly, she hobbled to the window and looked down at the courtyard. It had only been yes-terday that she was lying down there on a gurney, but it seemed like a lifetime ago. For a moment she was back in the basement, strapped down to the table as her kidnapper taunted and tortured her. At the sound of a rattling door knob, the memory receded, and she turned to see Adam strolling in, dressed in jeans and a fresh navy blue t-shirt and holding two lidded paper cups.

"Good morning," he said, holding one out to her with a smile. "Feeling any better?"

She took a careful sip. "My toes are killing me, but other than that..." she moved her arms, then turned her head side to side, "I think I'm okay. I take it they released you to go?"

"Yep." He stepped back and leaned against the wide window sill. "Tried to take me out in a wheelchair, even. I told 'em I couldn't leave quite yet. Had to wait to collect the rest of my valuables."

Claire felt the color rush into her cheeks as he winked and took a long drink of his coffee. She walked back across the room, suddenly very self-conscious of the thin hospital gown and the parts it didn't cover. Part of her wanted to be brazen, to find out what he'd do if she didn't hold the edges of the fabric so tightly together. To feel his lips on hers again, and his hands exploring her bare skin.

The other part wanted to slip into long pants and a turtleneck, hiding under layers of classy, modest clothing like she always did, distancing herself from those who couldn't believe she'd ever be anything more than her mother's daughter.

She settled gingerly on the side of the bed, noticing a large, yellowish bruise on her thigh. She prodded at it, surprised at how deep the ache went under the skin. Then the door swung open and different nurse in pink scrubs breezed in, smiling widely as if she had no other choice of expression.

"And how are we today, dear?" She handed a small white paper cup to Claire, and poured a cup of water from the carafe on the table. "It's just some ibuprofen for the pain - drink up."

"Thanks." Claire nodded, tossing back the pills. "Is it okay if I leave now? I feel pretty good, overall, and I'm sure Adam wants to get out of here."

"Let me check." The nurse went to the door and leaned out into the hall, then came back with a clip-board.

"Well, everything looks good, so I don't see why you couldn't go home today. I'll have the doctor sign you out, and you'll be free to go. I'll be back with some care instructions for those toes." She nodded and walk-jogged out before Claire could say another word.

"So you're all set then." That smooth, deep voice coaxed her gaze back to Adam's face. She couldn't have resisted if she tried. His head was cocked off to one side as he regarded her, and she wondered what he was thinking. "There's just one more thing we need to figure out before we go."

She frowned. "What's that?"

"Where we're going."

Someone knocked at the hospital room door, then slowly pushed it open. Claire grinned as Stacy poked her head in.

"Everyone decent?"

Claire shrugged, glancing down at her hospital gown. She sat back on her bed and pulled the blanket up over her legs. "As decent as I can get, I guess. But they're letting me out today - we're leaving in a little while. How are you feeling?"

"Much better, thanks." She put a shopping bag in the chair beside the bed. "I brought you some clothes, and you'll need to prepare a statement for the press. They'll be waiting when you leave." David came in behind her, nodding to Claire with a slight smile before joining Adam at the window. "Now." She put her hands on her hips. "I hear you need a place to stay."

Claire nodded, overwhelmed by the efficient way her friend just took over and started planning, as if nothing had gone wrong at all.

"Um, yeah, I guess so." She noticed that the guys had gone silent, and glanced past Stacy to where they were standing. Both had turned, and were blatantly listening to the conversation. "You heard what happened to my house, and Adam's house isn't really inhabitable either," she said, struggling to sort out the sudden panic she felt at the possibility of being separated from him. Stacy opened her mouth to speak, but Adam beat her to it.

"I've got it covered."

Stacy's eyebrows went up, her mouth curving into a wicked grin.

"I see."

Claire felt the heat rising in her face and avoided Adam's stare. Stacy dug in her handbag, then handed her a cell phone.

"You're going to need this. My number is in there - call me when you're in the lobby, and I'll get you through the press." She handed over a wrinkled piece of paper with scribbling on both sides. "Here are some ideas for your sound bites. Memorize them."

She turned to David and nodded, then turned away, her back straight and tall as she walked out the door.

Claire watched as David handed something to Adam. Then he nodded to her and strode quickly out the door after Stacy.

"So...that was weird," Claire said, frowning. Obviously there was still a lot going on between Stacy and David.

"They'll work it out." He came closer, letting a key on a plain ring dangle in front of her. "There's a little cabin on my parent's property - no one ever uses it, and you can't see it from the main house. We can stay there." His stare pinned her in place, and she knew he was offering more than just shelter. "If that's okay with you, of course."

There was uncertainty in his expression, shadows of the boy she'd fallen in love with all those years ago. He seemed to be holding his breath as he waited for her answer.

She tried to smile, to reassure him, but she

couldn't. Fear and desire warred within as she finally nodded, swallowing hard.

"Thanks - that would...um...be great." Her voice was raspy and she reached for the glass of water on the table, knocking it over with shaking hands. The plastic hit the floor with a loud crack, snapping the tension between them like a worn rubber band as water splashed all over Adam's feet. He flinched, and the shocked look on his face brought a grin to Claire's lips. She couldn't help it - she laughed.

Adam looked at her, one side of his mouth twitching upwards as the laughter kept coming. He gave in, chuckling, then shook his head and was at her side in two steps. He reached out to tilt her chin up with one hooked finger and before she could process his intentions he sealed his lips over hers in a possessive, searing kiss.

Chapter Six

Adam unlocked the door to the cabin and held the door open for Claire. Following her inside he flipped the light switch on, then locked the door. The living room was off to the left, a small square space with a dark green loveseat and two maroon chairs keeping watch in front of a large stone fireplace. To the right was a hallway that led to the kitchen, the master bedroom and a bathroom, and straight ahead was a narrow wooden staircase to the attic, where two tiny bedrooms had been tucked up under the eaves for David and him when they were kids. It had been a long time - he wondered if the *Ink* magazines he'd hidden between his mattress and box spring as a teen-ager were still there.

Claire stood still, waiting. Her shoulders were slumped, her eyes half-closed, and he knew that running the gauntlet of reporters outside the hotel had sapped what little strength she had left. A little food and a lot of rest was in order, now that they could relax for a few hours.

"Come on," he said, picking up her bag and leading the way into the hall. "There's a bedroom down here you can have - I'll stay upstairs." He pushed the last door on the right open and set the bag on an old cedar chest at the end of a white four-poster bed. "It's small, but you should be comfortable here. The bathroom is just across the hall."

Claire nodded, a wan smile on her lips. "It's fine," she said, hoisting herself up to sit on the tall mattress. She rubbed her face with her hands. "I should work on my notes for the debate tomorrow." Her gaze snapped to his, eye wide with alarm. "Oh no - we forgot Sly! We should go get him..."

"Sly's on his way." Adam grinned, moving to stand in front of her. "I asked David to pick him up and bring him over later. It's sweet that you're worried though, given how you feel about dogs in general." He cupped her face with one hand and leaned down to brush his lips over hers, then pulled back. "Are you hungry? I could make dinner..."

She shook her head, her eyes fixed on his chest. She reached out, hesitated, then grabbed the front of his shirt and pulled him close, locking her legs around his thighs.

"Adam, I --" He waited, pulse racing as she tilted her head back and looked up at him, her cheeks flushed and rosy. He'd never seen anything so innocently beautiful.

"Please, Adam. Kiss me again?"

All the blood rushed to his groin at her request and he groaned as she lay back on the bed, pulling him down on top of her. He nibbled at her lips as she ran her fingers through his hair and across his neck in a tender caress. She opened for him, her tongue darting out to meet his with the sexiest little whimpers that made him want to bury himself inside her, hard and fast. He kissed and suckled his way down her neck and across her collarbone, one hand sliding up her shirt to cup an ample breast. The feel of her hardened nipple against his palm made his cock twitch where it lay pressed against her core.

"Too many clothes," he murmured, pressing another kiss in the hollow of her throat. Pushing off the bed he pulled his shirt over his head as Claire made short work of her blouse and bra. Unable to resist, he dipped down and laved one of her dusky nipples with his tongue, sucking it between his lips as he ran his fingers down her belly to the waistband of her jeans. He undid the button and slid the zipper down, then tugged the material off her hips and to the floor where he knelt between her legs. The plain white cotton panties followed her pants and then he ran his hands gently, slowly back up the inside of her thighs, exposing her swollen sex.

"Beautiful," he breathed, unable to take his eyes

off of her glistening pink folds. He leaned in for a taste, swirling his tongue over her clitoris and she arched up with a cry, bracing her heels on the edge of the bed. Easing one finger and then two into her hot sheath, he closed his mouth over her tiny pink nub and suckled hard. She arched off the bed once more as he swirled his fingers inside her, a powerful orgasm rocketing through her body before she collapsed in a trembling heap.

Adam rose from the floor, kissing his way up her thigh, over her ribs and across her shoulders as he lay down behind her, pulling her into a close embrace. He held her while the tremors subsided, nuzzling her neck when she stirred. Feeling dampness on her cheek he frowned, rolling her onto her back so he could see her face.

Damn.

"What's wrong, sweetheart?"

A succession of quick taps on the window beside the bed sent Claire scrambling out of his arms and through the bedroom door. Adrenaline rushed through his system even as he slid off the bed, preparing to peek around the side of the thick drapes that had thankfully kept them hidden. A familiar baritone voice reverberated through the glass.

"Adam? You in there?"

* * *

Claire shut and locked the bathroom door, sliding down with her back against it to sit on the cool tiled floor. She heard a man yell somewhere outside and Adam replied with instructions to meet him at the front door. Footsteps padded in the hall, and stopped behind her, punctuated with the low thud of something hitting the floor. She wiped the tears off her cheek with one hand, hugging her knees to her chest as the knob rattled over her shoulder. In hindsight, she wished she'd grabbed her clothes on the way out of the bedroom.

"Claire? Are you okay?" Adam's low tone was gentle, caring even, and she wanted nothing more than to open the door and fling herself into his arms. Heat suffused her body remembering what he'd done, what she'd asked for. At first it had been amazing, wonderful, and then explosive. But after, when he'd pulled her to him and held her as if he really cared - it had been intimate. Too intimate.

"Claire?"

She exhaled slowly. "I'm fine," she said, thankful her voice sounded almost normal. The bathtub in front of her beckoned. "I think I'll take a shower, if that's okay." Some time alone would be good. Time to think and regroup. She waited, wondering if he'd gone. A door opened, then shut again somewhere nearby.

"I'll leave your bag and some towels right outside the door. When you're done, there's someone here I want you to meet. Someone I think can help." He paused, then she could feel his weight at her back as he leaned against the other side of the door.

"If I upset you, I'm sorry. When you're ready, we'll talk." He waited a moment longer, then left, his steps solid on the wood floor as he went towards the front door.

She sat still for a moment, wondering who the mystery man was. It would probably be more polite to just get dressed and forgo the shower for now rather than keep a guest waiting. She got to her feet, cautiously opening the door enough to grab the bag and two fluffy blue towels sitting on top before swinging it closed again. The events of the past couple of days played through her mind like a horror flick, and before she knew it she was standing under a strong stream of hot water, hoping that everything was just a dream and someone would wake her up soon.

Twenty minutes later, she finished re-taping her toes and opened the door, nearly tripping over a dark furry shape lying in the hall.

"Oh!" She stepped back, barely stopping her fall with a hand on the sink as the dog's tail thumped against the floor. "Um...hello Sly." His ears perked up, and he got to his feet, standing in the doorway with his head tilted to the side. She tried to stay calm, but pressure started to build in her chest, her breathing coming faster.

"Nice doggie?" She shifted her bag to hold it in front of her like a shield. Moving slowly, she took a step toward the dog, reminding herself to breathe. "Good boy. Just move back a little bit, okay? I don't want to hurt you, and you don't want to hurt me..."

"Sly. Come." The dog whirled immediately at his master's command and trotted down the hall, tail wagging like a plume.

Claire stepped out into the hall with a sheepish smile. "Thanks. I couldn't quite--"

"Don't worry about it." Adam's reassuring tone calmed her racing pulse. "You can work up to it. He doesn't hold a grudge." She looked down at the dog, sitting at Adam's heel. The animal certainly didn't look upset. She looked up again to find a tall blond man with huge muscles standing just behind Adam, staring back at her with an intensity that made her want to dart back into the bathroom.

Adam glanced over his shoulder. "Claire, this is Brandon, a friend of mine from college. Brandon, meet Claire Taylor."

"It's nice to meet you." Brandon stepped out from behind Adam, offering his hand with a half-smile. Claire slid her palm into his, grateful that he refrained from a show of grip strength. When he released her she forced herself not to back away, though the urge to flee was strong.

"I'll just wait in the living room," he said, nodding and then turned to go back down the hall.

She frowned at Adam. "I thought no one was supposed to know where we are. You said--"

"I called him from the hospital." Adam scratched Sly behind the ears, his relaxed demeanor doing nothing to assuage Claire's fears. "We need professional help on this, and he was in law enforcement for awhile. He runs his own investigating service now."

Folding her arms over her chest, she shook her head. "I don't like this. I get a weird vibe from him--something's off. I don't trust him."

"Brandon's a good guy. He's been through a lot though, and he's had to develop a hard attitude to deal with it that can turn some people off. Do you trust me?" Adam locked his gaze with hers, stepping closer into her personal space. Again she forced herself to stand her ground, her fingers tight on her arms to keep them from shaking.

"You said I inspired you once, you had my initials inked into your skin. Trust me now, Claire. I won't let anything happen to you." He reached out to run his hands over her upper arms, tugging her forward into his chest. He put his arms around her and she couldn't help melting against him, her hands circling his waist as she pressed her ear to his chest. She closed her eyes, listening to his heartbeat even as her head told her to keep her distance.

"Um...sorry to interrupt, but I think you guys should hear this."

Claire tried to pull away, but Adam slid one hand

down her arm, lacing his fingers with hers as he turned toward Brandon's voice. "What's wrong?" he asked, pulling her with him as he started down the hall toward his friend.

"David just got a call. Mel Dunham, his campaign manager hasn't been seen in over four hours, and no one can get a hold of him."

Stepping into the living room she saw David sitting on the couch and Stacy beside him, her hand on his shoulder. They both looked up, and Stacy dropped her hand to her lap.

"I think you should both drop out," she said, glancing quickly at David. "If neither of you are running, that should solve this whole mess, right? We could explain to city hall what's going on, and figure out who's behind all this before a new election is held."

"I'm supposed to throw the race." Claire's announcement rang hollow in the room as everyone turned to look at her. "That's what the guy who kidnapped me wanted - he said it would look weird if I just dropped out, but he wanted David to win, so he told me I had to stay in the race, but make sure I lost, or he'd kill me." Adam squeezed her fingers in silent support.

Stacy thought for a moment. "It could still work though," she said, standing up to pace in front of the window. "You could announce together that you're stopping the campaign, and recommending that the election be postponed."

"He'll know that I told David then," Claire said, shaking her head. "He'll still come after me. What I don't get is why he'd go after someone on David's staff. If he wants David to win, why would he want to take out his support group?"

Brandon straightened from where he'd been leaning against the wall, taking notes. "Is there any reason to believe that David is in danger?" Everyone looked at each other, but no one commented.

Claire shrugged, then shook her head. "I can't see why he would be, if the guy wants him to win the election."

He nodded. "I agree. I think David and Stacy should go home like normal, do whatever it is you were planning to do tonight, and Adam and Claire can hole up here. Cancel the press conference for now - the last thing we need is a public slip up to set this guy off." He waited until each of them nodded assent. "I'll do some digging, see if I can figure out what happened to Mr. Dunham, and we'll all meet back here tomorrow morning at noon. Does that work for everyone?"

"I guess we don't really have a choice." David stood, shaking hands with Brandon and Adam before pausing in the doorway.

Stacy slung her purse over a shoulder and got out her cell phone. "I'll cancel the press conference," she said, giving Claire a quick hug. "Hang in there, we'll get through this." She patted Adam on the shoulder and glanced at Brandon, then followed David out the door.

Brandon closed his notebook, then looked at Adam. "I'll call you when I've got something. I've got a few favors I can call in without raising too much suspicion."

"Thanks man, I appreciate it."

Claire hung back as Adam walked Brandon out, peeking out the front window to watch as the investigator got into a black Hummer and drove away.

* * *

Adam turned back toward the house as the vehicle rumbled out of site. Claire's eyes locked with his through the glass and a tingling sense of anticipation radiated out from her core. He moved through the open door, passing out of her sight for a too-long moment as she turned to watch him emerge on the other side. The locks clicked home and then he was looking at her, holding out his hand.

Asking. Inviting.

She hesitated. With Dunham missing and some sick madman using them all like puppets, it didn't seem quite right. There was also the matter of her heart, something this man had held for too many years to count. Allowing him to pleasure her earlier had been a mistake. She'd fallen for the illusion that he cared about her as much as she wanted - no, *needed*

- him to. That when this was over, he'd want to stay with her.

She watched him watching her, his patient eyes and relaxed posture calling to her on a deeper level. He would leave, of course. Her mother would say that was inevitable. All men left eventually. And so far, that was the one thing the woman had been right about.

For the first time, Claire found herself acknow-ledging how hard it must have been for her mother, constantly seeking that connection with someone the only way she knew how, only to watch it walk out the door over and over again. She'd never been strong enough to say no, and Claire had vowed never to be that weak. As she took one step forward, then anoth-er, until she was standing a mere breath away from the only man she'd ever loved, Claire finally under-stood.

She slid her hands up his chest, slowly curving her trembling fingers behind his neck and pulling his head down for a soft, hesitant kiss. His hands grasped her hips, pulling her tight against him as he sipped and nibbled at her lips. His arousal pressed against her belly, sending ripples of hot desire pulsing between her legs. He deepened the kiss, his tongue making love to her mouth and one leg slipping between hers, up to press against her molten center. A small gasp slipped past her lips when he moved his thigh just so, sending a little shot of electric energy back up to her hardened nipples, and he smiled against her mouth.

"Claire?" He pulled back just enough to look in her eyes, one hand gently stroking her back. "I need to be inside you, honey. I can't--"

She pressed three fingers against his lips, giving her head a little shake. "Shh...I want you too." She leaned in to place a light kiss at the base of his throat and then continuing up, angling her way up and across his neck to the base of his jaw. A low groan from deep in his throat vibrated through her body, and her pulse quickened as he slid his hands under her butt and lifted her off her feet. She wrapped her legs around his waist, savoring the feel of him nestled tightly against her clit while he carried her over to the worn couch and sat down, settling her on his lap. He reached under her t-shirt, pushing it up to expose the plain beige bra she'd pulled on underneath. Grasping the hem of her shirt, she pulled it off over her head. A small cry of disbelief followed as he reached back and unhooked her bra with one hand.

"Practice," he said, eyes alight with mischief. Then he pulled her forward, suckling one of her nipples into his eager mouth. "Mmmm."

Claire threw her head back, her eyes falling shut. His fingers felt like heaven as they splayed across her rib cage, holding her in place as he laved and sucked at each breast in turn. She wriggled, liquid heat between her legs begging for relief. "Adam?"

He nodded, not bothering to look up from where

he was placing kisses down the center of her chest.

"Adam, I need you."

He looked up, a tender, unfocused look in his eyes. "I'm right here - tell me what you need, Claire. Don't be shy."

He reached one hand up to brush her temple, cupping her face in his palm. His thumb stroked gently over her cheekbone and she tilted her head, leaning into his tender touch. Mesmerized by the adoration and hope in his gaze, she felt as though her chest would explode under the pressure building there. Swallowing hard, she struggled to find the words to tell him how much he meant to her. How much she wanted this. All of it. All of him.

"Love me, Adam," she finally whispered, a tear escaping down her face. "Just love me."

He tugged her to him, kissing her eyes, her lips, and down the column of her neck as he eased her onto the couch, slipping out from underneath her legs. Kneeling on the floor, he smoothed his hands over her breasts, lightly fanning over her nipples until they pearled hard against his palm. Claire arched up, offering herself to him and he accepted, rolling his tongue over one sensitive tip and then the other, his hand slipping down underneath the band of her sweatpants. Lower still, his fingers slid through her curls, finally swirling over and around her clitoris until her hips lifted off the cushion in a silent plea. She arched up again, closing her eyes as his touch between her legs became faster, more insistent. Laving his way down her belly, he pushed the fabric off her hips, nibbling lower until finally, finally his mouth closed over her hot core.

He plunged a finger into her wet sheath, and rolled his tongue over her clit simultaneously. Every muscle in her body contracted as the orgasm hit, waves of tingling impulses rolling just under her skin as he deftly pulled away. She whimpered at the loss, opening her eyes in time to watch him strip off his shirt, jeans and briefs. Her mouth nearly watered at the sight of his sculpted body.

He moved over her, his rigid cock probing gently between her legs before sliding into her wet heat. She sighed, lifting her legs higher to wrap around his ribs as he filled her completely. She held him in place with her ankles, reaching up to grasp his neck and pull his lips down to hers. He moaned as she thrust her tongue in his mouth, the sound making her pulse around him as he started to move inside her. Tearing his mouth from her he thrust harder, faster, reaching between them to press against her clit with his thumb just when she thought - knew - she couldn't take anymore.

The world went orange and crimson as her body arched once more in delicious pleasure and Adam pulsed once, twice, and again as he followed over the edge with a groan. He rolled to the side, pulling her into a tight embrace and she melted into him, his heart beating steadily under her ear as she nestled against his strong chest. Her breathing finally slowed, and she stifled a yawn, earning a deep, sexy chuckle in her ear.

"I should get you to bed," Adam murmured, shifting slightly in an attempt to extricate himself from the couch. Claire started to rise as he stood, but before she could get her feet on the ground, he bent down and picked her up, hugging her against his chest. She anchored her hands around his neck but kept her gaze lowered, the fears from before coming back in spades. She blinked against the tears welling in her eyes as he carried her down the hall and carefully put her down on the bed. Finally looking up at him, she saw a mixture of fear and indecision on his face as he reached for the covers they'd left askew earlier. Without a word he pulled them up to cover her, then leaned over to place a chaste kiss on her forehead.

Chapter Seven

"You should sleep," Adam said, running a hand down the side of her beautiful face as she snuggled under the thick quilt. Growing up, his parents had insisted he was too good for her, but he'd always known that wasn't true. It was the other way around.

"I'll be upstairs if you need anything." He turned to go, taking only a step before cool, trembling fingers closed around his wrist. Glancing back over his shoulder, he saw confusion and fear reflected in her eyes, glassy with unshed tears. Willing himself to be strong, he turned back, gently pulling out of her grasp to clasp her hand in his.

She swallowed hard, then licked her lovely red lips, still swollen from his kisses. An image rose unbidden in his mind of those lips wrapped around his cock, and he nearly groaned with need at the thought.

"Stay with me."

He should go. She needed to sleep, and he needed
to think. He hadn't expected this, hadn't expected her.
Would she even want him after all this was over?
When she went back to her life, and her political as-
pirations? Could he support that, when he couldn't
even support his own father and brother? She deserved better than that. She deserved the world. He'd
taught her that, without even realizing it.

She tugged at his arm, pulling him closer, her
knowing gaze hinting that she knew his thoughts.

"Please, Adam." Her voice was quiet but sure as
she came up on one elbow, the blanket dropping to
her waist and exposing those lovely smooth breasts.
"I need you."

Her fingers slipped out of his hand and tugged at
his hip, her eyes dropping to his hardening cock. He
allowed her to pull him forward, mesmerized as she
leaned in to touch the tip with her tongue. Electricity
jolted through him, and he instinctively thrust forward against her mouth, surprised when she made no
objection. Humming low in the back of her throat,
she swallowed.

His head fell back, eyes closed as sensations flew
through his body all at once while she suckled him
hard.

"God Claire *yes*," he rasped as she released him
with a wet, popping sound. He took a deep breath,
looking down at her just as she started to lave his rod
with her tongue, long hard strokes licking from root

to tip as she stared up at him with innocent eyes. It was easily the sexiest thing he'd ever seen. He buried his hands in her hair, holding it out of her face and steadying her as he started to thrust slowly in and out of her rosy lips, the fantasy becoming reality as he touched the back of her throat.

She urged him on, nails digging into his butt as he moved faster, her gaze locked solid with his. Her mouth tightened around him in time with his thrusts, the sensation making his balls tighten in anticipation. Close. He was so close, and he tried to pull away, but she held him in, reaching up to give a quick tug on his sack, triggering a release so strong he staggered against her. His seed spilled down her throat and she swallowed every last drop, then slowly released him, licking her lips like a satisfied cat.

"Adam?" He stared at her, trying to remember why he should leave. "Come to bed, Adam." She flipped the covers off her glorious body as she scooted back to make room. Smiling shyly, her cheeks blushing pink, she patted the bed beside her.

He lay down and gathered her up close, his heart tight in his chest as he drifted off to sleep.

* * *

Adam groaned, opening his eyes to a black void as a loud, insistent jangling noise rattled through his head. Warm softness filled his palm and he squeezed gently, kissing Claire on the shoulder before he eased away from her. Rolling over, he picked up the heavy old receiver next to the bed, and made sure the cord pointed down before placing it to his ear.

"Cranston."

"Sorry to wake you, man - but I've got information on David's campaign manager. It's not looking good. Can I come by?" The solemn tone of Brandon's voice brought Adam more fully awake, and he swung his legs over the edge of the bed, rubbing his face with his other hand.

"Yeah. We'll be waiting. Is Claire in danger?" The bed squeaked slightly as sheets rustled being him. He turned slightly to find Claire sitting up, her shape barely visible in the pre-dawn light, holding a sheet up to cover her torso.

Brandon exhaled long and low. "Not this minute, but yeah. This is serious shit. I'll be there in twenty."

Replacing the handset, Adam looked back at Claire. Her hair was tousled, her teeth nibbling at her lower lip. It took all his restraint not to reach out and pull her into his arms, but he couldn't resist leaning in for a quick, reassuring kiss.

"We need to get dressed-- Brandon's on his way. He's got news." He stood, finding his jeans in the dark and pulling them on, watching as she scooted to the edge of the bed still primly holding the sheet up.

"What time is it?" she asked, starting to pull the sheet with her as she moved to walk past him. He reached out and flicked the white material out of her grasp, wrapping an arm around her waist with the other.

"Early." He leaned down, and suckled gently first at one nipple, then the other. Ripe for his touch, they pebbled under his tongue before he straightened to look in her eyes.

"You have a gorgeous body," he said, taking one last taste of her abused bottom lip. "Now get dressed." He grinned at her confused frown, stepped back and smacked her on one smooth buttock with an open palm as she turned away, earning a soft squeal.

Chuckling, he pulled on his shirt and headed for the door, turning back in time to catch her caressing the spot where his hand had just been with a small grin. Interesting. Filing that tidbit away for later, he walked down the hall to make coffee and watch for Brandon's truck.

* * *

Claire heard the door to the bedroom close and let out a long, slow sigh. Grateful for the darkness that hid a furious blush, she gathered her sweats and shirt, briefly contemplating putting them on without underthings to save time. Quickly discarding that idea, she felt around for her bag, loathe to turn the lights on just yet. She slipped on a clean pair of panties and a bra before dressing, wondering when she'd become so wanton. She'd never been brave enough to seduce a man before, and never with *that* sort of thing. They always came to her. Always. And oh lordy. She hadn't really enjoyed that slap on the ass just now, had she? That was the sort of thing prostitutes and strippers liked, not strong, independent women. Wasn't it?

Biting her lower lip, she glanced at the door. She'd have to go out there and face him eventually, but how could she act normal? Her nipples still ached after his tender kisses, her breasts feeling full and heavy. Her face was hot, and probably beet red. Brandon would know what they'd been doing. Guys always seemed to know.

"Claire?" Adam's voice carried through the door from somewhere down the hall. It wasn't a lover's voice though, but rather stern and focused. It was what she needed to mentally pull herself together, and she took a deep, settling breath before pulling the door open as he called out again.

"Brandon's here. You'd better see this."

She padded down the hall, stopping just long enough to get a band from the bathroom to pull her hair back. The men were sitting at the small kitchen table, and both looked up when she entered. The smell of brewing coffee made it seem almost normal to have a guest at Several photographs lay on the shiny wood surface between them. Moving closer, she frowned as she tried to reconcile her own image with the images below the hand-drawn markings. She picked one up to examine closer, her heart speeding up as it finally came together. Her neck in a noose. Her face in a plastic bag. Her back bearing angry, bleeding slashes. Her chest red with some sort of black markings covering the surface.

"That's me."

Brandon nodded. "These were found in Mel Dunham's apartment."

"There were more. A lot more." Adam stood and pulled out a chair for her. "Here, sit down. I'll get the coffee."

She put that photo down, picked up another. On some level she was horrified, but all she felt on the surface was numb. What kind of a person wanted to do such horrible things to another human being? Brandon reached over and tugged the photos from her, arranging them neatly and placing them in a manilla folder. Only then could she draw a full breath.

Adam came back, three steaming mugs in hand. He placed one in front of her, and handed the other to Brandon before taking his seat.

"Are you okay?" He stroked her arm with long, soothing motions.

"Just shocked," she finally managed. "Those were in his house?" She looked up at Brandon, his eyes soft with compassion. "Why? Why me?"

He shrugged, taking a sip of coffee. "Hard to say. Have you ever had much contact with him?"

"Not really." She glanced at Adam, and he squeezed her hand. The simple movement jogged a dormant memory, and she sat up straight, suddenly awake.

"Actually, he hit on me in high school - grabbed my hand at lunch one day, and wouldn't let go. It was creepy." Adam tried to pull his hand back, but she held tight. "Now that I think about it, he was at my college too. It's odd that I never really noticed before."

"He didn't want you to notice." Brandon tapped two fingers on the file. "Guys like this want to be in your life however they can. If you reject them, which I assume you did, they'll just slip in under the radar. You're lucky he hasn't done anything until now." He frowned, looking down at the table. "I can't figure out why he let you go though. That doesn't make sense. It was the perfect opportunity and he blew it."

Claire took a sip from her cup, the bracing liquid flowing like sludge down her throat just as a loud crash sounded overhead.

Hot coffee sloshed down the front of her shirt when Claire twitched at the noise overhead. Sly's bark resonated from the living room and chairs scraped harshly against the laminate floor as both men stood. Brandon moved quickly out into the hall, drawing a gun from the waistband of his jeans.

"Stay here," Adam said, his tone firm. "It's probably nothing, but we need to go check. She nodded,

and he squeezed her hand lightly before he followed
Brandon through the doorway. She took a towel from
it's place on the stove handle and halfheartedly
rubbed at the brown stain on her shirt with shaking
hands. Tossing the towel into the sink, she went back
to the table and sat with her back to the wall, staring
anxiously at the door as she listened to them pounding up the stairs, Sly's incessant barking adding to the
chaos.

The small chandelier above her shook as footsteps
traveled purposefully across the ceiling. There was
small comfort in knowing where they were, even as
she sat alone gripping the edge of the table. It didn't
make any sense that Mel would be here though. He'd
had his chance to kill her earlier, but he hadn't. In
fact, he'd seemed far more interested in making sure
David won the campaign than in her personally. She
was just a means to an end, or so she'd thought.

Glancing up, she realized the noise had stopped.
A stair creaked, then another. She watched the doorway, gripping the edge of the table hard. Why was it
so quiet?

"Adam?" she called out, pushing her chair back
from the table until it met the wall. "Brandon?" When
no one answered, she eased off of the seat, the hair
on the back of her neck tingling. Something was
wrong. Where was the dog?

There was a door to her right that she assumed
led outside, and she inched along the wall toward it,

grasping the cool knob with her right hand. Her eyes never wavering from the narrow view into the hall, she pulled open the door and slipped inside, pulling it silently closed behind her. It was pitch black, and her heart pounded as she turned and stretched her hands out, feeling shelves and cans on all sides. A lump formed in her throat as panic tightened her chest. She was trapped.

Hearing steps in the kitchen, she held her breath as shadows moved across the slim band of light at the bottom of the door. If it were Adam or Brandon, they would be looking for her, calling her name. She stood perfectly still, briefly wondering if the pantry door hand a lock. Closing her eyes, she tried to picture the outside of the door, but it was no use. She hadn't paid enough attention earlier to remember. Ever so slowly she reached out, searching for the knob with her fingers in the dark. Maybe if she could just feel...

The barest touch of her skin on metal was all she felt before the door swung open, bright light from the kitchen blinding her as she instinctively pulled back.

"Hello, Claire."

Chapter Eight

Claire blinked, her vision blurry in the bright kitchen light. She didn't need to see to know who had discovered her in the pantry though.

"What are you doing here, Mel?" she asked as his face slowly came into focus. Round and bald, his head resembled a shiny bowling ball, his eyes and nose perfectly spaced for the holes. He reached out to lock stubby fingers around her wrist and pulled, surprisingly strong for his chubby physique. She stumbled over the low threshold and lost her balance, falling heavily against him. Caught off guard, he went down backward, pulling her with him to the floor.

"You're going to pay for that," he growled. She fought to get away, gaining her feet only to be yanked back down by one ankle.

"Adam!" She kicked out, her heel making contact with something hard as she tried to crawl closer to the door. "Brandon!"

Raspy laughter came from behind her just as she managed to wrench her foot free.

"I'm afraid your protectors have fallen asleep on the job," he wheezed as she stood and ran to the hall. "If you leave, I'll simply take them instead," he called, his voice fading as she reached the stair case. She glanced back at the front door, then took the stairs two at a time up to the second floor.

A black mask of some sort lay on the floor at the top of the stairs and she wondered briefly what it was for as she jogged by, opening each door in the hall and scanning the rooms until she reached the last one. A small window was propped open on the back wall, and a faint sweet smell wafted past. Pushing the door open, a blast of the same sweet smell hit her full in the face, and her mind struggled to understand why Adam, Brandon and Sly all lay on the floor at her feet.

The world started to spin. She lost her balance and fell to her knees, only vaguely aware of feet shuffling behind her before everything went dark.

* * *

Adam woke to nausea and a throbbing headache, made worse by the incessant shrill whistling coming from the other side of the room. His arms and legs were bound to the hard wooden chair he sat in, and his feet were bare on the cold floor. With consider-

able effort, he turned his head to survey his surroundings. It was a basement or a garage of some sort, with
concrete floors and walls and a long wooden work-
bench attached to the wall around the perimeter. Mel
Dunham stood at the far end, his back turned as he
moved shiny metal objects around, arranging them in
some sort of pattern on the bench. But it was the
sight in the center of the room that incited rage in his
soul.

An autopsy table sat underneath a bright spotlight, a large bucket under the head catching the
drainage hose. Laid out on top with her neck suppor-
ted by a thick white block was Claire, still dressed in
sweats and a t-shirt, her hair pulled up to cascade over
the end of the metal platform. He stared intently at
her chest, looking for any slight movement, praying it
wasn't too late.

"Oh good," Dunham said, startling Adam from
his vigil. "I was waiting for you to join us. Now we
can get started."

Adam rolled his head from side to side, pretending to stretch his neck as he looked for anything in his
immediate area he could use as a weapon. Dunham
was smart. The floor around him was clear, the
closest pile of junk five feet away on a low table.
Looking up, he knew he had to draw attention away
from Claire for as long as possible. Her chest rose
and fell on a shallow breath, thank god. At least she
was still alive.

"Why didn't you just kill her the first time?" He looked Mel straight in the eyes, interested when confusion, then frustration crossed the man's face.

"That wasn't me," he growled, shaking his head at the floor as he walked around the table and crossed his arms over his chest. "Although I did punish the offender, and spent a little time with our girl before putting her in the courtyard. He should never have touched her. She's mine. She's always been mine."

He looked up then, moving closer as he leaned down, scowling. "You never should have touched her either. That's why you're here, you know." He glanced over his shoulder, staring at the table before turning back, his eyes glassy and unfocused. "It's not all your fault though. I saw her seduce you. I saw her mouth wrapped around your...well. The damage is done now. Time for you both to pay for your sins."

He went back to the table and leaned over Claire, smoothing a hand over her forehead before taking up a short knife and cutting down the center of her shirt. Adam strained against the ropes holding him down, moving his wrists and ankles side to side checking for weak spots as he watched Dunham spread the shirt open, revealing a plain white bra covering Claire's breasts.

"I think you'll appreciate this part, but you'll understand that I can't let you get to close," Mel said, moving to the other side of the table without looking back. "If you look up and to your left, you'll see a screen where you can watch."

Adam looked up as a black screen flickered to life, and Claire's face and chest came starkly into view. A low, familiar hum filled the room as he stared at the purple outline that started at the base of her throat with the letters M and D in a stylized format connected by two chain links, and more purple chain circling either side of her neck in a thick ink necklace.

"Do you think she'll like it?"

He forced himself to look away from the screen to find Mel watching him with obvious delight. In one hand, he held a shiny metal tattoo gun attached to an air hose. Adam's stomach twisted as the man bent over Claire and touched the tip to her skin. He jerked his head back to the screen, sick at the look of terror on Claire's face as her eyes flew open and she whimpered at the pain of the needle piercing her skin. Adam winced at what she must be feeling. Aside from the helplessness at being tied to the table, tattoos always hurt more the less fat there was under the skin. He continued rubbing the ropes against the chair, unable to look away as Mel carefully followed the purple pattern on Claire's skin. He had to get to her before Dunham started on the chain links at her neck if there was any hope of her not being publicly branded for life. Even now, she'd have to wear high collared shirts to cover the design. He refused to think of what else Dunham might have planned.

The rope at his wrist broke, finally, and he worked

his hand out of the binding, then reached down to loosen the ties at his ankle. Dunham turned away for a moment, and Adam quickly undid the knots on his other side, leaving the ropes in place for now. A few more strokes with the needle and Adam tensed, waiting for his chance.

The next time Dunham turned Adam moved quickly, reaching the other side of the room in several long strides. He wrapped his arm around the other man's neck, squeezing hard as Dunham jabbed the tattoo gun into his forearm. Wrenching away, Adam turned and grabbed the closest item on the bench, swinging wide at Dunham's head. The hammer connected with a grotesque crack, and Dunham fell to the floor, blood pooling underneath him as the tattoo gun hung from the bench, still humming.

"Adam? Are you okay? What's going on?"

"I'm okay," he said, leaning down to pull the foot pedal that ran the gun out from under the table brace. The humming stopped, leaving them in cold, damp silence as he went to Claire's side and began to release her bonds. His hands shook and he took a deep breath, knowing he had to compose himself.

For her.

"Just be still for another minute, if you can. I need to put something on that wound."

She nodded, her gaze following his every move as he worked around to her other side. Her eyes were glassy and she shivered as he found a clean cloth and some ointment to put over the new design. When he would have stepped away from the table for a moment, she reached out and grabbed his wrist hard.

"Don't leave me," she said, her voice breaking. "Please."

"Shh. I'm here." He tossed the ointment tube over to the bench and then bent down, cupping her face with his hands. "It's okay. I've got you. I promise I'll never let you go."

Tears slid down her face and he kissed them away, one side then the other, finally pressing a tentative kiss to her lips. She opened for him, her tongue meeting his in a dance that sealed the connection between them. Sliding an arm under her knees and another under her back, he reluctantly pulled his head away.

"Don't look down," he warned, and she hid her face against his neck as he carried her away from Dunham's corpse.

* * *

Two weeks later, Claire sat at a long conference table at City Hall with Adam on her right and Stacy on her left. David and his mother, the elections administrator and Mayor Thomas completed the group. After Adam had saved her and killed Mel Dunham, he'd taken her straight to the police and they'd reported the whole story. It hadn't taken long for the press to get a hold of it, and soon the Elections office had been besieged by requests to delay the election until she and David could regroup. The current mayor had called them both and requested a meeting to give his decision before the press was notified.

He cleared his throat, glancing at each person before resting his gaze on Claire. "How are you feeling, Ms. Taylor?" His tone was gentle, and she fought the urge to rub the base of her throat. The skin had healed over, but every time she looked in the mirror she was reminded of Dunham, and how close she'd been to death.

"I'm fine, Mr. Mayor." Forcing the corners of her lips up, she inclined her head slightly. "Thank you for asking." Adam laid his hand over hers, the gauze that still wrapped his own injury soft against her skin. He'd been lucky that the needle had missed hitting a vein, but it was still a very deep wound, and he'd been fortunate that infection hadn't set in.

"And the case is closed - there's no further danger?"

She nodded. "That's correct. Dunham is dead, along with the man who kidnapped me in the hospital."

After they'd finished telling her story to the police, they'd learned that a body had been found in the basement the day Dunham had made his move. The man's dental records had matched a hit man who had carelessly kept the number for David's father in his wallet. The ex-politician had been arrested and was awaiting trial in jail. It had been hard on David, and while he wouldn't talk about it, Claire knew it was just as hard on Adam knowing his father had hired someone to kill her. Or at least threaten to kill her if she didn't drop the race.

Mayor Thomas leaned back in his chair, pulling the reading glasses off his nose and tossing them on the table. "I have to say, this is very unusual. But due to the public outcry, it has to be addressed. But I can't just hold off the election. Federal laws are the prime authority in this case, so I'm afraid my hands are tied." He sat up, lacing his fingers on the table.

"The only thing I can do is remind you that neither one of you actually dropped out of the race. While I can't postpone the election, you're both welcome to start campaigning again and your names will be on the ballot. But I'm afraid that's the limit of my authority in this matter. If you both withdraw, we'll have no choice but to have the city council appoint someone to fill the seat until another election can be held, since my term is up and I'm not eligible to run again."

Claire looked across the table at David. His expression was stoic, punctuated by harsh lines and dark half-circles under his eyes. She wasn't sure if he intended to continue the campaign or not. Stacy had tried to call him for the past week, but he wouldn't take her calls, and he'd refused to talk to Adam as well. He'd effectively shut himself off from the world, with only his mother for company.

A light squeeze on her hand brought her attention back to Adam. He raised his eyebrows, silently urging her on. She let out a long, slow breath, then met the Mayor's steady gaze.

"Thank you for your reassurance, sir. I've decided to withdraw from the campaign," she said, her voice sounding much louder in the room than she'd intended. At her announcement, Stacy stood and took the formal letter she'd drawn up earlier to the election administrator. "I don't think I'm in any position to lead the city right now." She chuckled low, shaking her head as she looked down at the table. "I don't even have a place of my own, much less any money to run a campaign with. I might run next time, but for now, I need to pick up the pieces and start over."

Lifting her head and pushing her chair back, she met David's cold gaze as she stood up. "I don't blame you for your father's actions. I just wanted you to know that. I think you'll make a great mayor." Adam's hand was warm in the small of her back, and she let him lead her out of the room, leaving the others to wrap things up.

* * *

Several hours later, she opened her eyes as Adam switched off the bright overhead lamp, and chewed on her lower lip. Pushing herself up to sit on the edge of the his work table, she took the hand mirror from him and examined the fresh ink he'd laid over Dunham's letter blocks. Already her skin was red and becoming puffy, but the intricate vines and flowers that he'd somehow woven into two interlocking hearts took her breath away. Squinting, she tried to find the original lines and letters Dunham had left, but there was no trace. Tears spilled down her cheeks as she lowered the mirror, meeting Adam's kind eyes on the other side.

"Are those happy or sad tears?" he asked, worry crinkling the sides of his face. She laid the mirror behind her, then reached for him, pulling him in close for a kiss.

"Definitely happy," she replied, pressing her lips against his once more. He pulled back and she grinned up at him, swiping at her eyes with one hand. "It's beautiful. Thank you."

His arms came around her waist and he pulled her up tight against him, careful not to touch her new cover-up job. "It was my pleasure, though I'm sorry it had to be so conspicuous. If I could have stopped him--"

"Shh." She kissed him again, soft and teasing. "No more of that. You're a hero. My hero. Now kiss me again."

"Yes ma'am." He smiled, leaning in to press his lips against her forehead, then the tip of her nose, sending a delicious shiver down the back of her neck.

He nuzzled his way down her jaw line, and she sucked in a breath, prepared to beg if she had to.

When his mouth finally came down over hers, she sighed, wrapping her legs around his waist. "I love you," she whispered against his lips, praying he wouldn't push her away. She trembled as he brought one hand up to cup the side of her face, a tender look in his eyes she'd never seen before.

"I love you too." The words tattooed her heart just as surely as he'd marked her skin.

About the Author

A full-time webmistress by day, Jamie DeBree
writes steamy, action-packed romantic suspense late
into the night. Her goal is to create the perfect blend
of sensual attraction, emotional tension and fast-
paced adventure, similar to the television crime dra-
mas she's hopelessly addicted to.

Born in Billings Montana, she resides there with her
husband and two over-sized lap dogs. She reads in a
wide variety of genres including romance, erotica,
action/adventure, thriller, horror and literary.

For information on upcoming books, visit
jamiedebree.com.